DIRE HAPPENINGS
AT SCRATCH ANKLE

DIRE HAPPENINGS
AT SCRATCH ANKLE

Celestine Sibley

HarperCollins*Publishers*

HarperCollins books may be purchased for educational, business, or sales promotional use. For information, write HarperCollins Publishers, Inc., 10 East 53rd Street, New York, NY 10022.

FIRST EDITION

Designed by George J. McKeon

Library of Congress Cataloging-in-Publication Data
Sibley, Celestine.
   Dire happenings at Scratch Ankle / Celestine Sibley.—1st ed.
     p.   cm.
   ISBN 0-06-017703-9
   1. Women journalists—Georgia—Atlanta—Fiction. 2. Atlanta (Ga.)—Fiction. I. Title.
PS3569. I256D57 1993
813'.54—dc20
                                      93-8985

93 94 95 96 97 ❖/HC 10 9 8 7 6 5 4 3 2 1

This book is dedicated to James A. Mackay, his daughter and law partner Kathy, and their friends Jim Youmans and Ken Pennington. They introduced me to the beauties and perils of northwest Georgia and the excitement of rappelling and caving. They are, however, in no way responsible for any errors I have made. I know that they will forgive me and I hope that all the other people who know and love Dade County will forgive me for the liberties I took with its geography, especially moving the courthouse from Trenton to Rising Fawn, and populating it with purely fictional characters.

Dire Happenings at Scratch Ankle

CHAPTER ONE

KATE MULCAY HAD not covered Georgia politics in a long time and she didn't particularly want to. The calling had become pallid and self-righteous. There hadn't been a voting scandal of any scope since a south Georgia county had collected votes from a cemetery full of tombstones in a long-ago governor's race. There hadn't been a memorable sex shocker since a much-married governor had declined to divorce his wife and marry his pretty young mistress when she became pregnant but had smiled on her tenderly, called the state patrol, and asked them to send a trooper over to marry her.

Wicked. Shocking. Kate agreed, but it had sure made newspapering interesting and as she sat in the Georgia House of Representatives chamber that winter afternoon, she thought a little malefaction wouldn't be bad.

The old chamber was tired. It was getting on toward the end of the forty-day session and Kate wondered if the skipper of this old ark, Speaker Frank Pitts, had not long since dispatched a dove to the outside world and seen it come winging back with an olive twig in its beak, indicating mellow weather in life beyond the capitol.

Kate sighed and tilted back in the press section swivel chair and looked around. On the other side of the glass that segregated the press, the people's representatives appeared listless and bored. Some of them read the afternoon paper. Some of them were furtively cleaning out their desks against the time not many days off when the Speaker's gavel would fall and he would intone the final words of the session: "This House now stands adjourned sine die!" Then, according to custom, the members would fling a snowfall of papers into the air, let out a fusillade of Rebel yells, and, jostling and backslapping, work their way out of the capitol toward their respective homes in Georgia's far-flung 159 counties.

Kate was the only newspaper reporter she knew who had genuinely enjoyed covering the General Assembly. When other people were removed from that assignment, they heaved great sighs of relief and treated the press-room corps to celebratory drinks. When Kate was ordered back to the office to write an editorial page column, she mourned at cleaning out her desk in the pressroom and turning it and her telephone over to a lanky kid newly graduated from the University of Georgia's journalism school.

Being in the capitol in lawmaking season was, to Kate, to be in the heart of the state and intensely alive. She found herself homesick for the place, the tall chamber with its long windows now heavily swathed with draperies

2

but once open and looking out on the capitol lawn, with its blooming borders and old gray monuments and with pigeons preening dingy feathers and cooing along the window ledge. She delighted in the ancient rituals of law-making borrowed from the British Parliament. The daily bit of theater when the members recessed for the night and the Speaker left the podium and went to the floor and bowed to the left, bowed to the right, and ran from the chamber was one of those remnants of the past that unfailingly pleased Kate. She liked the fact that the Governor could only enter the House by invitation, like the British monarch and the House of Commons, and she enjoyed the clarion call of the doorkeeper from the center aisle, "Mistah Speakah! His excellency the Governor of Georgia asks permission to enter the House of Representatives!" In a way it was playacting; in a way it was a nice nod to the past and Mother England with a sort of Magna Carta flavor. Most of all, Kate liked knowing the members, most of them leaders in cities and country towns from all parts of the state. In her day at the capitol the membership was exclusively male, except one session when there were a couple of women members battling to get their sex admitted to jury duty.

There had always been a sprinkling of elegant, old-fashioned orators whose speeches were rich in imagery and eloquence. There were also "wool-hat boys" with the flavor of the soil in their speech and the courthouse crowd back home dictating their every move. Kate enjoyed them all.

She remembered with affection the old retired postmaster from a little south Georgia county whose one and only appearance in the well of the House was to defeat a bill to erect a monument to the brutal Confederate commandant of the infamous prison camp at Andersonville.

The old gentleman, silver-haired and blue-serge-suited, had been shy but invincible. He told the still somewhat chauvinistic House that his grandfather had been a Confederate soldier assigned as a guard at Andersonville prison and had personally witnessed and been sickened by the atrocities committed by the commandant, Major Henry Wirz, against Union prisoners. His grandfather had never forgotten cruelties to helpless prisoners of war which, he contended, ranked alongside Hitler's brutalities.

He spoke in the quiet, courteous tone of a grandfather reasoning with recalcitrant grandchildren. Then he gathered steam:

"Honor that fiend with a monument?" he cried. "Oh, the shame, the disgrace to our state and the honorable men who fought for the Confederacy! I beg you gentlemen to show that you deplore such heinous atrocities. I beg you to reject this resolution!"

And then, lifting his faded old blue eyes to the House ceiling, he echoed that southern hero Patrick Henry: "A monument to Henry Wirz? Forbid it, Almighty God!"

He sat down, pink-faced and flustered, to a storm of applause. Kate heard later that he had gone home and had a fatal heart attack, but he had defeated the effort to honor a sadist, even one who happened to be wearing the gray.

Now back in the present-day House chamber listening to the reading clerk's singsong litany about some land dispute somewhere, Kate wondered if there were any shy, brave old gentlemen down there at the little Victorian desks with their glowing maple spindles and lift-lid tops. The current membership looked generally young with smart blow-dry haircuts, conservatively tailored suits, and the sheen of higher education on their brows. More than that, they were considerably diluted with blacks and women.

Kate rejoiced in the high incidence of women and blacks entrusted with the people's business nowadays, but as a reporter she mourned their lack of color—and humor. They took themselves and their jobs seriously. They knew that the day when the electorate cherished clowns and cutups was long gone, and rightly so. But Kate couldn't help it; she missed the rogues and scoundrels, but most of all the funny ones.

There was the representative who was an undertaker "back home" and tried to camouflage his dolorous calling by wearing loud plaid suits with electric bow ties. He had a whole rainbow of loafers in colors to match every outfit.

"I'm just a dirt-road sport," he had remarked to Kate one time in wry self-assessment.

And there was the exuberant, bombastic old-timer who wasn't in his accustomed seat on opening day. His name was missing from the roll call. Wondering about him, Kate found him, listless and lonely, in the capitol coffee shop and asked him the reason for his absence.

"Oh, I didn't come back," he said morosely. "For reasons of health. The voters got sick of me."

It wasn't likely that any of the current crop of lawmakers talked like that, Kate thought. She heard them sometimes on television and they were always earnest and usually self-congratulatory.

She wondered how the reporters who succeeded her could abide them. Then she noticed that one of the few reporters remaining in the press box this late in the day, a fellow named Gary Boone from the afternoon paper, was sound asleep. And the gorgeous blonde who represented one of the television stations was catching up on her homework for whatever degree she was seeking at Georgia State. They all had so many degrees, Kate thought guiltily. She had been a college dropout. But they didn't seem to be savoring the Georgia General Assembly as she always had, before a new city editor, thinking he was promoting her, misguidedly transferred her to columnizing. Anyhow, the legislature seemed to have lost its pizzazz.

The reading clerk fell silent and the Speaker said, "Chair recognizes the gentleman from the First."

A tall lean young fellow with dark eyes in the murky hollows of a bony face and a shock of black hair was approaching the well of the House. Kate idly checked her legislative directory. She didn't expect much of him or of any of the proceedings this dull day. She was only there filling in for Johnny Weaver, the regular capitol reporter, whose wife was having a baby. He had told her nothing much was coming up, but Shell Shellnut, the city editor, running her in as a substitute, said, "Any little thing,

Kate. I doubt if there'll be a good murder for you, although God knows we'd welcome anything. News is nonexistent today."

"I can skip the murder, Shell," Kate said, putting on her jacket. But she knew Shell didn't believe her. She had helped her late husband, Homicide detective Benjamin Mulcay, investigate so many murders, her colleagues on the paper pretended to believe it was a major hobby with her.

Clearly there would be no murder in this somnolent lawmaking body today. Members seemed as drowsy as her neighbor in the press section. But the gentleman approaching the microphone in the well of the House did look tense and keyed up.

She found his name in the little directory: Rep. R. Pickett. That was brief. Most members listed a couple of given names and often a nickname.

Her neighbor, Gary, was coming to life, already seasoned enough as a reporter to have that built-in automatic response to action on the floor.

"Who is this?" she asked.

He yawned. "Return Pickett. Indian warrior. They call him Turn."

"He does look like a Native American," Kate admitted.

"He's no more native than the rest of us," Gary said, yawning again. "He's a freshman and he's been on the warpath ever since he got here. The boys"—he nodded toward the floor—"are getting tired of it. But I think the female members consider him sexy and they think it's kind of a nice change when he's down there looking at them with those haunted bedroom eyes."

7

"What's his cause?" Kate asked.

"Oh, you know, the same old dead horse they've been beating for years. They must have been at it when you covered the capitol. Tennessee is stealing Georgia blind."

Kate looked startled and then she remembered. There had been a recurring rhubarb about some land in downtown Chattanooga that was part of a tract that belonged to Georgia's state-owned railroad. It had become valuable—to Tennessee—commercial property. That was an ancient legal hassle that had been mediated half a century ago. But what now? Suddenly she started laughing. "Not the General again, is it?"

Gary shook his head. "You mean Walt Disney's *Great Locomotive Chase*? I don't think so. I wasn't here, but I believe Pickett said the courts gave that one back to Georgia. It's in a museum around the Kennesaw Mountain battlefield somewhere, I believe."

Kate nodded.

The little wood-burning locomotive had been stolen by a party of plainclothes Union spies while its Confederate crew breakfasted at a place called Big Shanty on the road to Chattanooga. The Confederates chased them on foot and by handcar and an unexpectedly appropriated engine or two, finally retrieving the little engine just short of the Tennessee line. The Union raiders fled but were subsequently caught and hanged. Many years after the war, Georgia leased the little train to the Louisville & Nashville railroad for show purposes and it toured the nation, returning to the South, where Tennessee laid claim to it with such enthusiasm and affection that it was on exhibition at Tennessee's newly renovated depot and medals of it were struck for souvenirs. Chattanooga's mayor had its likeness emblazoned on his official stationery and even the city's fire trucks wore pictures of the General.

Georgia went forth to battle once more, this time in the courts, and finally the little engine came home. There was bitterness in Tennessee. Some women wept and swore they would never cross the state line into Georgia again, even to shop.

It couldn't be at issue again, Kate thought, turning her attention to the young man at the microphone.

She could see why women in the capitol regarded the representative from the First as sexy. He had that lean, rangy Gary Cooper build with a bronzed face and those dark eyes that gleamed with a fanatical fire. A long bony hand chopped the turgid air of the chamber and his deep voice rumbled over a theme about rape.

"Rape, did he say?" asked Gary, come to life again.

"I think rape of the land," said Kate.

"Oh, that," said the young reporter, slouching back in his chair. "He talks about that a lot. His ancestors were in the Trail of Tears."

That sad old drama, a blot on the state's history which citizens had been shamed by and had grieved over for more than a century and a half, Kate mused. The Cherokee Indians had lost their homes and lands in north Georgia and had been driven to a government reservation in the West, a death march for thousands of them, now dramatized as the Trail of Tears.

But it was over and done with in 1838 or '39, so what was there to be said about it now? She listened attentively.

"And I say to you, ladies and gentlemen," the young zealot thundered, "my people were robbed of their homes—murdered, robbed, raped. And it is happening again! I submit to you that history is repeating itself! Georgia is being invaded. The state line is a joke, a farce. We have lost once more the lands of my people. Even before the infamous Trail of Tears my ancestors had cause to weep tears of blood. Their very graves are on alien soil."

Gary Boone stirred restively. "Here we go again. Dragging Canoe."

"Dragging what?" asked Kate.

"Oh, some old Indian chief," Gary said. "Turn's great-great-great-somebody. He's obsessed."

But the young man in the well didn't look obsessed now. He was silent for a moment and smiling slightly, an almost shy, crooked smile that showed a flash of very white teeth.

He was gathering steam for the finish.

"I'm asking this House," he said with sudden gravity, "to pass this resolution calling for realignment of our state's northern boundary, to send a committee from this General Assembly to see what injustice is being done to our citizens, and to report back that we may, ladies and gentlemen, *act!*"

He made as if to resume his seat, but then he turned to the microphone once more.

"You all know that beautiful mountainside, that Eden, that heaven on earth that artists call Plum Nelly. It was a fun name meaning that it was 'plumb out of Tennessee and nelly out of Georgia.' That was back when a little woman named Fannie Mennen lived and painted there on beautiful Lookout Mountain. But, my fellow members, if we don't move fast, that wondrous spot called Plum Nelly will be plumb out of Georgia and plumb *in* that state to the north of us!"

"So what?" mumbled Gary, getting to his feet and preparing to leave for the pressroom just as a voice in back of the chamber cried, "Mister Speaker! I move that House Resolution 389-983 be recommitted to the State Institutions and Property Committee for further study!"

Representative Pickett paused on his way back to his seat and looked stunned as the House by voice vote promptly shelved his resolution. Not so Native American that he didn't register disappointment, Kate thought, getting to her feet. Impassivity must have been bred out of Dragging Canoe's great-great-great-descendant.

Back at the office Kate learned that there had been another protest march about replacing the Confederate battle flag as the state flag and the photo department had come up with some fine pictures of people in shabby Confederate uniforms marching and singing in a cold drizzle of sleet and rain. Shell wanted to play them big, so there was not much room for Representative Pickett's resolution and not much interest, either. Feuding with

Tennessee and sometimes with North Carolina was old stuff that had had its day.

As Kate walked away from the city desk, Shell called after her: "Say, what is this Plum Nelly? Who's this Nelly broad?"

"Aw, Shell," Kate said with a laugh, "don't you know 'nelly' is the approved southern pronunciation of 'nearly'?"

"No, thank God, I came from Ohio," said the city editor, pushing Kate's story to one side.

But Kate, on her way to her log cabin home in the woods twenty-five miles north of Atlanta, could not get the young legislator with the fierce eyes off her mind. Was he nuts, or did he really have something besides the ancient Cherokee grievance to base his resolution on? It wasn't much of a story, after all these years of the bickering, which the newspaper faithfully covered. There were some legislators, busy with more urgent matters, who privately said Georgia was paranoid on the subject. Kate smiled to herself, remembering that the coastal ones fought to save the famed "Marshes of Glynn"; the city ones fought new soft drink taxes, which would be bound to alienate that reliable benefactor, the Coca-Cola Company; and the ones from the tobacco belt raged against additional cigarette taxes as if they would undermine pure drinking water and southern womanhood.

Each to his own, Kate thought, turning down the dirt road that led to her little cabin. The sight of her cabin, as always, caused Kate's heart to lift with affection and pride. The weathered old log walls looked welcoming in the light of the setting sun. They had survived a century and a half of summer suns and winter rain and sleet, and Kate always fancied that their shabby gray and lichened runnels and furrows held some of the color and life of the passing seasons. She and her late husband, Benjy, had found the cabin, long deserted and dilapidated, twenty years before his death.

Together they had shored it up and made it as snug and comfortable as its old shake roof and the gaping spaces between the logs permitted. It was small, but it accommodated their books and the country possessions of old cupboards and braided rugs they had loved and painstakingly acquired at auctions and old house sales through the years. Now Kate lived in it alone, and as she parked her car and walked toward the kitchen door, she thought of the young legislator named Return. Maybe he had such a feeling for home. She stopped to pat her almost-Dalmatian dog named Pepper, who rushed out to meet her, and paused as she pushed the kitchen door open to speak respectfully to her white cat named Sugar, who, against house rules, dozed on the old homemade hunt board where her mother's yellowed and veined ironstone tureen held a bunch of forsythia branches she was trying to force into early bloom.

One day, she thought, Sugar would knock that tureen off the table and break it.

"You do that," she threatened him, rubbing his ears, "and I'll give you to the subdividers."

It was a much smaller loss and invasion, she thought,

than the one Representative Pickett's ancestors, the Cherokee Indians, had suffered when they were driven off their lands, but she thought she had an inkling of how they felt when developers had arrived in her woods and populated them with elegant million- and half-million-dollar houses.

She kicked off her shoes, got a beer out of the refrigerator, and made a resolution. *Tomorrow,* she decided, *I will talk to Mr. Pickett.* Crazy and illogical as his attempt was to take back lands belonging to the neighboring state of Tennessee, at least there was feeling there, perhaps akin to her own profound feeling for home. There had to be a story or maybe a column in it.

The next day was Friday and the legislature adjourned early. Kate caught Representative Pickett as he wandered, looking lost, up the splendid marble stairway to the capitol's fourth floor. "You going to look over the museum?" she asked him. He nodded gravely.

"There are things that belonged..." He paused and gulped, and a slight flush touched his high bronzed cheekbones.

"Oh, yes," said Kate. "I remember pottery and arrowheads." She grinned to show she was making a joke. "Are you going to ask that those be returned, too?"

The young legislator, surprisingly, smiled back and Kate once again admired the flash of white teeth in the dark face. "You think I'm bonkers, don't you?"

"I don't know," said Kate frankly. "I thought it might

be a strong feeling for home and I understand that, loving my own primitive digs."

"I know you live in a log cabin," the legislator said, surprising her again. "I've read about it in your column. Maybe my people built it, you know. The Cherokees lived in houses instead of in tepees."

"No, you can't claim my house," Kate said firmly as they reached the stop of the stairs. "I know its history. White settlers came over the mountains from 'Ca'lina in kivered wagons' and cut the logs and hauled the rocks and built it themselves five or six years after . . . don't you call it The Removal?"

"Probably on Cherokee land," Pickett said dryly. "But don't worry, I won't contest your right to it. I would," he said with his crooked smile, "like to see it someday." And then to answer her question: "Yes, the government called it The Removal, but Trail of Tears is more accurate. You do know that it was one of the most barbarous, cold-blooded crimes in this country's history?"

Kate nodded. "I saw the pageant up in North Carolina one summer. But you can't undo what happened a hundred and fifty years ago, you know."

"Read the history books," the young man said. "You'll see the greed and hatred that led to it and . . . " he paused in front of a painting of an Indian chief in a fine feathered bonnet, "you'll see the kind of cruelties I think you can never forget. Four thousand or more people died, many of them children. My great-great-great-grandmother carried her dead baby for two days before she let them bury it on alien land in Tennessee."

"Is that why you are resuming that old fight with Tennessee?" Kate asked.

The afternoon light slanting down from the capitol's gilded rotunda touched his shining black hair and dark face, which seemed to have an underlayer of crimson.

Redskins, they called them. Incongruous for such a well-tailored, well-barbered young man. Only his rugged half boots suggested that he might be an outdoorsman.

"Did you grow up on the reservation?"

"Born there," he said, "and named Return because they hoped I'd come back and avenge them."

"But Tennessee?" said Kate. "I thought most of the Cherokee Nation was in Georgia."

"I live here," he said, "in the Free State of Dade. I hope to bring family members back to Rising Fawn to live where our ancestors lived, hoping they will reclaim some of their land. If I marry, I hope I will have children who will feel a blood affinity for the land, especially that area now claimed by Tennessee but which is in reality Georgia's. Our ancestor, a chief, lies there—in alien soil, his grave unknown."

"Dragging Canoe?" Kate ventured.

He lifted his black crow's-wing eyebrows. "How did you know?"

Kate shrugged. "I guess we've had stories."

"He was a very brave man," said Pickett. "A great war chief. Different from another forefather, Attacullaculla. You've heard of him?" Kate shook her head. "He was a peace chief, who fought on the side of the white man,

16

even going to England to meet the king as a child. He hoped for peace. He signed a treaty giving millions of acres to whites, but he warned them. Ah, he warned them!"

The dark head tilted upward; the dark eyes examined the rotunda. "He told them," he said softly, "'You have bought a fair and beautiful land, but you will find its settlement dark and bloody.'"

Standing there among the museum's cases of tattered flags and stained and worn uniforms from four wars, Kate shivered a little. It was as if one of the snakes from the wildlife case a few feet away had slithered toward her. So many wars, so many turbulent upheavals had come to the "fair and beautiful land," wars not just Cherokee in origin. The peace chief's words sounded like a curse— and she didn't believe in curses.

She tried for logic.

"Do you think it's reasonable to change the state line, at probably great expense, to satisfy the remembered wrongs of a handful of people?"

"I do," said the young man. "For more reasons than that. The first and foremost is that it's right."

"Well," conceded Kate, "you can't beat right. Or can you?"

"You can try," said Pickett somberly. And then he smiled. "Why don't you come up to the State of Dade and let me show you what I'm talking about? I could meet you in Rising Fawn early Saturday morning."

The name of the little town was so beautiful Kate was

tempted. Or maybe she was tempted by the strange attraction of the dark young man named Return.

"I'll have to see," she said tentatively.

"In the meantime," he said, "it's getting late and the traffic is still heavy. Why don't you let me buy you a drink? Firewater."

Kate laughed. "For an Indian you are mighty knowledgeable about some of our better white customs here at the capitol. Newspaper reporters and some members of the General Assembly often do what we call 'waiting out traffic' at the end of the day by having a beer at some gracious hole in Underground Atlanta. I never heard them call it 'firewater,' however."

"I went to Georgia Tech," he said, "but I cling to a few archaic expressions."

Waiting out traffic took an hour and Kate found herself in the curiously partisan position of wanting to believe Representative Pickett. (Only now she was calling him Turn and he had stopped putting the "Miss" before Kate.) They parted by the big fountain outside Underground. He said he was leaving for Rising Fawn and Kate promised to meet him there early Saturday morning. It is a town so magically small, he had said, smiling proudly, that when she arrived inside the city limits he would most certainly know it. But to be sure, she could park on the main street and he would see her, if she had not already spotted his dusty red pickup truck, which would also be parked on the main street, probably in front of Miss Pearlie's Café.

Maybe he was bonkers, as he had suggested, Kate thought as she climbed the steps to Whitehall Street and threaded her way through fruit carts along the curb, past the Five Points MARTA station toward the newspaper office. Maybe there was no story there, as Shell indicated in the office, but it wouldn't hurt to see. She was looking forward to seeing Turn again, even if he was in the grip of an obsession, and after all, for all her travels over the state for the newspaper, she had somehow missed Rising Fawn. Such a pretty name, she mused, a town named for a Cherokee councilman, Turn had said, who was by Cherokee custom named for the first thing his parents saw after his birth. His father had looked out of their house at dawn and seen a beautiful baby deer struggling to stand on its slender legs at the edge of the clearing. Rising Fawn, beautiful name—and when the baby grew up he became a respected Cherokee representative in the Indians' dealings with the whites, Turn had said.

Back at the office, Shell, as Kate had anticipated, settled for a couple of small stories she had on General Assembly actions but rejected Representative Return Pickett's crusade.

"The customers get tired of the same old state line feud year after year," he said. "It stops being news."

Kate found she wasn't tired of it. She called Reference and was lucky enough to get Richard, a young fellow who didn't weary of history. Did he remember Georgia–Tennessee squabbles over anything besides football? she asked impudently.

"Sure do," said Richard. "What can I send you?"

"Anything you've got on boundary disputes."

Within a few minutes a pneumatic tube from Reference plummeted into a basket in the newsroom and Kate hurried over to see if it had her name on it. It did, and she took out a sheaf of copies of stories going back to the 1950s and stuffed them in her briefcase. She would read them when she got home.

On the way up the expressway toward her cabin in north Fulton County she found the name Rising Fawn running through her head. A poem? A song? When she reached the turnoff at Roswell she remembered it—a poem a long-ago southern poet had done in the style of Stephen Vincent Benét's ode to American names. His name was Daniel Whitehead Hicky and his poem had gone:

> O, Dewy Rose and Talking Rock.
> O, rain-wet Rising Fawn.

There was more saluting such Georgia names as Social Circle and Ty Ty and Ringgold. She couldn't remember how it went, but from her own knowledge of Georgia's geography she bet Georgia place names could outpicturesque the rest of the country's, except possibly Mr. Benét's line, "Bury my heart at Wounded Knee." She thought he might have liked Benevolence and Enigma and Between and Doerun and Flowery Branch and Dooling and Deepstep.

The Hicky poem had ended:

May all the names I love best
Drift back in music over me
For one who loves each door, each lane

... What else? It didn't matter. She was turning in her own lane, approaching her door. She would have a bath, find something to eat, and settle down to read the clippings in her briefcase in preparation for meeting Turn.

There was a light on in her kitchen and her heart sank. The Gandy sisters—Sheena, age twelve, and Kim Sue, eleven—must have preceded her. Pepper had not even come out to meet her. Some watchdog, she thought irritably. Probably on the sofa being cosseted by the girls.

It wasn't quite that bad. He was under the kitchen table on which the Gandys had spread a jigsaw puzzle which they appeared absorbed in, while their feet stirred around in Pepper's salt-and-pepper hide, alternately roughing it up and smoothing it, a most delectable treatment for a dog.

"Well, girls ... " began Kate helplessly, "what are you doing here?"

"Um," said Sheena, fitting a piece of red rooftop in place, "we come to see you."

"We didn't even light the fire," said Kim Sue smugly. "We knowed the danger."

Kate had forbidden fire-lighting in her cabin when she wasn't at home. At least they had obeyed that rule. But still...

"Look, girls, I love you and I'm always glad to see you, but I think you'd better run along home tonight. I have some reading to do and I leave early in the morning for Lookout Mountain. I need a bath and a bite of something and then I have to get busy."

"Aw, shoot," said Kim Sue, her freckled face downcast as she carefully sustituted the word "shoot" for the word she knew Kate disapproved.

"We told Mommer you'd just as soon have us as not," the older sister, Sheena, explained bleakly.

"Ah, you know I always love to have you," said Kate, putting an arm around each pair of skinny shoulders. "But tonight . . . well, Lookout Mountain is a sort of working trip and—"

"Lookout mounting?" Sheena repeated the destination like it was nirvana. "You going all the way up yonder? We ain't never been up there."

"We had a cousin went onct," put in Kim Sue.

"Said it was mighty educational," interposed Sheena, knowing Kate's high regard for learning—at least for them.

"Well, yes, I suppose it is," said Kate tiredly. "But now you all scoot. I need a bath."

"Yes'm," they said dolefully, brushing their puzzle into its box and turning toward the door.

"Have a good one," Kim Sue offered politely.

"See you later, alligator," said Sheena.

Kate smiled but pointedly refrained from playing their after-a-while-crocodile game. They didn't need any encouragement, and as much as she loved them and valued their help in solving a neighbor's murder a year or so ago, there were times when she valued most being alone.

Two grubby little country girls, the descendants of one of the last old farm families left in the settlement when the subdivisions came, they were fine in their way, but there were times when if Kate couldn't have Major Benjamin Mulcay, she wanted no one. After a marriage of twenty years, it was sometimes easier to adjust to nobody than to somebody.

She climbed the narrow steps to her bedroom and began divesting herself of her town-going work suit, piling everything on the bed and kicking her shoes under it as she headed for the bathroom and a shower. Once, over the sound of the water—which sometimes gushed and sometimes trickled, due to the idiosyncratic plumbing done by a man whose specialty was homicide detection—she heard a stirring on the stairs. She attributed it to Pepper and went on lathering herself.

When she came out, wrapped in the pride of her meager linen closet, a sheet-sized towel, she found her suit on a hanger, suspended from the closet door, and her shoes side by side on the little rack put there for the purpose.

"What on earth?" she muttered, and peered over the stair rail.

The Gandy sisters sat together on her sofa, a zipper bag, which they often brought for overnight visits, between them.

"Girls?" she said ineffectually. "You're back."

"Yes, ma'am," said Sheena. "Mommer's got to go hep midwife our aint. She's having her seventh young'un and the doctor won't come no more. She said it wasn't no telling how long it would take and we just as well go with you."

"Besides," said Kim Sue, "we ain't never seen Rock City. She says it's near 'bout as good as Disney World."

"Oh, but I'm not going to Rock City," protested Kate. "It's the other end of Lookout Mountain where I'm going."

"It don't matter," said Sheena soothingly, as if Kate were apologizing. "Same mounting. Couldn't be far."

She stood up. "We fixed you some supper. Come on and set down."

Kate was touched that they had made her a peanut butter and jelly sandwich, placed it neatly on one of her best plates, and lined up precisely beside it a bottle of beer. Was her pleasure in an occasional beer so noticeable the children thought she had to have it? She pushed it aside as she picked up the jelly-dripping sandwich before she realized she was still wearing nothing but a towel.

"Wait a minute, I'll light the fire," said Kim Sue, who was a junior-grade pyromaniac anyhow.

"And I'll git you a josie," said Sheena, using the country word for any covering garment. She headed for the stairs.

Kate chewed peanut butter, jelly, and slightly stale bread and looked at the girls helplessly. She couldn't send them home if their mother had gone off to midwife for their "aint" and she wasn't certain how Representative Return Pickett would feel about them horning in on his tour of onetime Cherokee lands.

It didn't matter, she decided after a while. The weekend was her time off from the paper and if she chose to go sightseeing with the Gandy sisters, it was her own business.

She smiled over her sandwich at the two freckled faces. "Did you bring enough clothes for two days?" she asked.

The Gandy sisters, realizing that there had been a change in the climate, wriggled with delight. "Yes, ma'am!" they said together. "The jeans we've got on are clean and we brought dresses like you like for church."

It was both a concession to her archaic churchgoing habit, Kate realized, and assurance that they were ready for any exigency.

"Okay," she said, yawning. "Jackets because it's going to be cold and tough shoes for climbing rocky places. Got it?"

"I think they got their paths paved at Rock City," Kim Sue offered in a small hopeful voice.

"Hush up," ordered Sheena. "Miss Kate may not be a-going to Rock City."

"No," said Kate, now that she had been pampered with supper and a fire and a robe, deciding to mollify them. "We are going to a most interesting spot very few people in Georgia know. It is said to be the smallest and one of the most beautiful counties in the state. It used to be called the 'lost county' because there was no Georgia road leading to it. You had to go to Tennessee or Alabama to get there.

"There's a legend that when Georgia was slow to secede from the Union before the Civil War, the people of Dade County went ahead and voted themselves out of the United States. They didn't get back in for eighty-five years. They called this county the 'Free State of Dade.'"

She could tell her little guests weren't mesmerized by her history lesson. To give it a little glamour she added, "They had a party when they decided to return to the Union and it was on the radio all over the country!"

Her audience brightened, but not much.

"Not the teevee?" asked Sheena.

"Didn't have it then," said Kate. "That was a long time ago on the Fourth of July in 1945."

The girls were yawning. Kate shooed them up to bed. They would sleep on her bed and she would get a pillow and cover and bed down on the sofa. It would be easy to read there by the fire anyhow.

The girls fought spiritedly over taking turns in the bathroom. Although subdividers had paid a nice chunk of money for their grandfather's old cornfield, in a burst of reverse economy the Gandys had opted for two automobiles instead of one bathroom.

Once she had tucked her guests under the old quilts, some inherited from her mother, some given to her by their neighbor, Miss Willie Wilcox, she got a pillow and a comforter and settled on the sofa by the fire.

The story she had just told the girls about Dade's secession from the United States was widely believed and a favorite of hers, but she knew it was of dubious historical accuracy. Nevertheless, the people of the county liked it and, according to one of her clippings, citizens of the mountainous county "from Sitton's Gulch to Wildwood" came down from the hills to the county seat of Rising Fawn to vote for and celebrate "the return of Dade" to the Union.

Lot of "returning" around here, Kate said to herself as she shuffled her clippings. First the whole county and now one lone, very appealing young man. Kate wished that at her age she wasn't so susceptible to handsome young men. When she looked in the mirror, always accidentally, and saw her fast-graying hair, her sagging jawline, and the crow's feet around her eyes, she knew that they thought of her as a mother or grandmother figure and that wasn't at all the way she felt. It wasn't that she aspired to romance. Benjy had provided that. It was just that she didn't feel so far gone into age that she couldn't have a pleasant conversation, drink, or even an evening with a young man if he was interesting.

Return Pickett, now, what was he, about thirty or thirty-five? Younger? She couldn't tell, but their time in Underground was no-age. She even thought it would have been agreeable if he had held her hand a moment longer when they parted. Then she looked at her hands: rough and red from wood-getting and gardening, short nails, a callus on one forefinger, and freckles—or were they what the ads used to call "horrid age spots"? *Ha,* she jeered at herself. Nobody would ever hold one of those hands again!

She turned her attention back to the clippings. Georgia and Tennessee and possibly even North Carolina got into a land squabble as early as 1818 when a surveyor, according to legend, got drunk and drew the Thirty-fifth Parallel, making the state boundary too far south. Nothing was resolved then. One story in 1964 quoted the state attorney general as saying sixty square miles of land, including valuable deposits in the area of Copper Hill, rightfully belonged to Georgia. He was prepared to file suit in the U.S. Supreme Court to reclaim it, but the then governor decided litigation would be too costly and directed the attorney general to drop the matter.

Was that the land Return was pushing the legislature to retrieve?

The "return" commanding the most newspaper space and generating the most emotion was the return of the little Civil War locomotive and Kate was tired of that, even if the president of the United States, then governor of Georgia, Jimmy Carter, welcomed the General home in 1972.

She sighed and dropped the clippings to the floor and pulled up her comforter. Too bad Return didn't want something that would capture the public imagination like a little locomotive. What did he want? How many acres? Where? Most of all, why? Would the descendants of the Trail of Tears come trailing back?

Kate punched her pillow and drew up her feet, which were always cold when she slept on the sofa, and eventually slept.

Getting Sheena and Kim Sue up and dressed and on the road the next morning in the predawn darkness was not much trouble. They still harbored the delusion that they were going to Rock City.

"I remember when we had a birdhouse that said, 'See Rock City' on it," Kim Sue said dreamily.

"You do not," Sheena contradicted her. "We never had no birdhouse in our family except some tacky old martin gourds."

"Well, I knowed somebody who had 'See Rock City' painted on the roof of their barn," Kim Sue persisted. "Was pretty, too. They got to go see it free for having it painted on their barn."

"My," said Kate absently, looking for the exit to Dade County. "That would be nice."

"How far is Rock City from where you got to go?" Sheena asked after a long silence.

"Honey, I don't know!" wailed Kate in exasperation. "I think it is a long way. Lookout Mountain is a very big mountain—about ninety miles long."

There was silence in the backseat for a mile or two and then Kate heard Kim Sue whisper, "I'm so hongry I a-perishing!"

Kate had anticipated that.

"Here," she said, throwing back two packages of Oreo cookies. "That'll do you till we get to Rising Fawn. The man I'm supposed to meet said they have good breakfasts there. How about hotcakes and sausage?"

The girls weren't thrilled, but they were quiet.

They passed through a little settlement with a funny sign Kate pointed out. "Look," she said, "'Exciting Naomi'! We are entering 'Exciting Naomi'! Look at it and tell me what you see. Is it really exciting?"

"If you ask me," Sheena said judiciously a moment later as they left Naomi, "they are trying to pull our leg."

Kate ransacked her mind for another diversion.

"When I was your age," she said, "we used to always sing on car trips. Let's sing. What do you like?"

"Miss Kate, you know you cain't sing," Kim Sue pointed out. It was so true Kate had to laugh. She loved to sing, but she knew this pair came from a long line of country music makers and had no patience with her tuneless croaking. They didn't even know the songs she liked—jolly camp tunes from her own childhood, Cole Porter and Irving Berlin songs to court by, church hymns. They probably were too young for Bing Crosby and Perry Como.

"Well, let me hear you all sing," she said. "It will cheer me up for a long working day." She was to recognize the fantasy in that later.

They were launched on something about a snow white dove when Kate hit the main street of Rising Fawn.

There was no dusty red pickup truck in sight. There were a few cars and trucks in front of Pearlie's Café, where Kate, mindful of the "perishing" girls, parked. It was early. She would take the girls in for breakfast where Turn would easily find them.

Pearlie was a plump lady wearing a blue sweat suit and eye shadow to match. She greeted Kate and the girls enthusiastically and found them a table by a window where they had a good view of the street.

"Have you seen Representative Turn Pickett this morning?" Kate asked as they were seated.

"No, I haven't," said Pearlie. "He must be a-lawing in Atlanta."

"I don't think so." Kate made her contradiction polite. "The legislature is in recess for the weekend. He said he would meet us here this morning."

A man with a group at a big table in the middle of the room spoke up.

"You must be that newspaper lady from Atlanta. Turn told me he was expecting you. The pretty little girls threw me off. Wasn't expecting them. But we're mighty glad to have them. Why don't you all come and sit with us over here? This is the community table. Turn always sits with us."

Sheena and Kim Sue were pleased to be asked and went over, flipping their stringy, sun-faded hair back with the air of models preening satin tresses.

Kate followed them.

"I'm Kate Mulcay," she said. "These are my neighbors, Sheena and Kim Sue Gandy. And you . . . ?"

"Pauling Merritt, called PawPaw," said the big man, standing and extending a surprisingly soft and well-manicured hand. "This little lady over here is Edie Putnam, and these rascals"—waving at two young men— "are Joe and Frank Priestley. Whit there"—pointing at a young man in a green jumpsuit—"used to be a forest ranger, so we call him—guess what—Smokey."

The little girls gasped.

"Did you ever see Smokey the Bear?" asked Kim Sue boldly.

The young man pushed a green hunting cap up on his head and smiled.

"Yes, ma'am," he said. "We are big buddies."

"Oooh!" breathed Kim Sue. "Could we see him?"

"Might," said the man, "but he's usually sleeping this time of year."

Everybody smiled benignly on the little girls and PawPaw pulled out chairs for them and for Kate and called to Pearlie, "More grub, hon. I bet these Atlanta folks is starving for a good breakfast."

Nice people, Kate thought happily, looking around the table. Edie appeared to be the youngest, a tanned piquant face and blond hair cropped short. The Priestleys—brothers, she supposed—had startlingly blue eyes, and such hair as she could see around the edges of the caps they didn't remove at table was fair. Their hands, which only briefly let up manipulating their forks as PawPaw made the introductions, were tanned and work-callused.

"This is a regular breakfast club?" she asked, and Edie explained.

"Most of the men around here come every morning. Some of us can only make it on Saturdays. I teach school. We're cavers and we're planning a big ridge walk today, hoping to check out a couple of unexplored caves. A lot of others will be along shortly."

"And Turn, is he a caver, too?"

"Was," said Smokey, "but he got hurt rescuing a girl who was rappelling out of control over on Pigeon Mountain and his leg hasn't healed too well."

"Limps," said Pearlie, putting plates of grits and eggs and country ham and biscuits before Kate and the girls.

"He'll be back with us sooner or later. He's especially

interested in caves on the Tennessee side of the mountain," one of the Priestleys said.

"I just met him at the capitol the other day," ventured Kate, "but I didn't notice that he limps."

"Hides it pretty well," said Jim, one of the cavers, "until he gets real tired and it starts hurting bad."

Kate buttered a biscuit and let her eyes rest on Edie, wondering if she was Turn's girlfriend. Pretty, probably still in her twenties, and apparently the kind of steady sensible girl men liked.

"Are you the only female caver?" she asked.

"Gosh, no!" said Edie. "The wives of these fellows come with us when they can park their kids with grandparents, and there's always a crowd from Atlanta. We have a woman pediatrician and a woman police officer and one of our best is a beauty. Former Miss Dade County."

No end of possibilities for the handsome Turn, Kate thought, leaning over to cut Kim Sue's ham and push the fig preserves back from Sheena's plate. "When does Turn usually get here?"

"'Bout always early," said a Priestley, looking at the big watch on his wrist.

"Yeah, usually beats us all here," said Smokey. "Says he likes to get Pearlie's first making of coffee."

"Aw, you know how it is," said PawPaw. "Send a feller to Atlanta and he gits himself a set of new ways. I bet Turn is over yonder in his trailer sleeping in."

"Ringing for room service," joked Smokey.

They all laughed and PawPaw stood up and reached for the check.

"Oh, no," said Kate. "That's mine. You were good to let us join you, but I can't let you buy our breakfast."

"Company, ain't you?" said the big man. "We always try to feed up company. Next time, you or your boss down there at Atlanta newspapers can treat." He ruffled the girls' hair and they giggled.

"Let him have it," said Frank. "He's our tycoon. Or do you call that typhoon? Anyhow, he's the richest man in town."

Kate took another look at PawPaw's jeans and plaid shirt under what could have been a very expensive sport coat and his peaked cap with BUD emblazoned across the front. *They're kidding me,* she thought. *Big business doesn't dress like that.*

Edie's eyes were fixed on her with a glimmer of amusement in their amber depths. "Is," she murmured, and then added, "Would you like to look around town and view our views while you wait?"

"Yes, thank you," said Kate. "That would be wonderful."

Outside the restaurant the group stood a moment, looking at the great blue silhouette of Lookout Mountain rising above them. The valley was still swathed in mist, but the mist was, they all agreed, lifting as the eastern sky lightened and the sun stained the clouds with rose and gold, proof that it was rising over there somewhere.

Edie suggested that they go in her Blazer, a perky little half truck, half station wagon. The girls climbed in enthusiastically.

The business street was quiet. The half dozen stores had not opened, but a teenage kid was hoisting the flag in front of the brick post office and Edie stopped and lowered her window.

"Hi, Ira!" she called. "How's your granny?"

"Tolerable," said the boy. "She's coming in to open up, but she can't rest till this flag is flying. She'll put up the mail herself. Always does."

He got the flag to the top of the pole, secured the rope, and as they drove away Kate saw that he stood back and saluted it.

"He's one of my brightest students," Edie said. "Eagle Scout, too."

The girls had turned in the seat to watch him and they murmured together, "I pledge allegiance to the flag of the United States of America . . ."

Sometimes a strange and illogical affection for them welled up in her and brought a dampness to Kate's eyes. *Little brats*, she thought. *Wonderful little brats.*

The sun was now almost full out, making the mountains that encompassed the valley more blue than violet.

"We'll go by Turn's place first," Edie said. "He lives on old Scratch Ankle Road in a trailer in a very pretty spot." After a moment she added, "'Bout the prettiest spot on Scratch Ankle."

"What a fine name," mused Kate. "Indian in origin?"

"No," said Edie. "I've always heard miners gave it that name. It is a trail down to the old coal mine and it used to be all grown up with the most vicious briars you ever saw. Miners went to work and went home so mutilated by the thorns they were bloody. They named it."

The road climbed to a rocky shelf overlooking the valley and Edie slowed the car to let them see the view. Then she turned abruptly down a winding dirt road.

"Scratch Ankle?" Kate asked.

"Almost," Edie said. "Leads to it."

Pines and hemlocks and rhododendrons crowded close to the road and made a dark canopy over it. It crossed a narrow rocky trail and came out in a clearing. There, with its back to a wall of tremendous gleaming rocks, stood a neat trailer, freshly painted and with small Burford holly bushes anchoring it to the ground. An old whiskey barrel by the walk held a mass of cold-defying pansies. A red pickup truck stood in the yard.

"I guess he's here," Edie said, tapping her horn. Nobody appeared. "Maybe he is still asleep or out walking in the woods. I'll go see."

She walked to the door and started to knock, but she found it ajar. Pushing it open and calling his name, she stepped inside. Kate heard her scream and within seconds she was back in the open door, white-faced and trembling. Kate scrambled out of the Blazer and ran to the trailer.

"Blood," stammered Edie, retching. "Blood everywhere. You look."

Kate brushed past her and into the small foyer. There was an immaculate kitchen on one side. Across from it the door opened into a small living room. Kate started in and then stopped, aghast. She closed her eyes for a second to shut out the appalling sight. A sofa covered in gray tweed was drenched with blood. There was blood on the floor and blood on a crushed lampshade on the floor and on the lamp base that stood on a table at the end of the sofa. A small Navajo rug in front of the sofa was streaked with crimson.

A pile of papers on the floor at one end of the sofa seemed to be still wet with blood. Kate took a step forward, involuntarily reaching for them. And then she backed off. As the wife of a homicide detective she should know better than that. As a reporter she had an overwhelming desire to examine them.

"The sheriff..." she faltered. "We should call the sheriff. The phone..."

"In the kitchen," said Edie. "And there's one in the bedroom, too."

Kate heard the voices of the little girls approaching the trailer.

"Oh, God," she moaned, "make them go back." Then she called to them, "Sheena, Kim Sue, get back in the car! I'll be there in a minute! Go sit in the car!"

Then to Edie, "We must not touch anything in here. Is there a neighbor anywhere close?"

"Not close," said Edie despairingly. "And if I move the car, won't that mess up any tracks in the yard?"

"You're right," said Kate. "Let's use the kitchen phone." Turning from the bloody room to stand in the doorway where the cold wind from the mountain swept in, she said, "You call. You know the sheriff."

She heard Edie dial and she watched the girls dragging their feet toward the Blazer, where they leaned against the hood looking sulky.

"Why cain't we see, too?" Kim Sue complained.

"'Cause it's prob'ly another murder," muttered Sheena.

In the kitchen Edie chokily asked for the sheriff. Kate turned to listen, waiting because she was afraid the young schoolteacher in her shock and—was it grief?— might topple over.

"He's coming," Edie said, turning from the phone and leaning against the door facing.

No! Kate started to say. There might be fingerprints there. Instead she said, "Let's go wait in the car."

She put an arm around Edie and led her across the yard to the Blazer. Kim Sue and Sheena were not in it.

"Oh, my lord!" she cried. "They'll fall off the mountain! Sheena! Kim Sue! Where are you? Come back this minute!"

There was a rustle in the bushes next to the road and the girls came out, holding aloft a bitter weed.

"Look what we found by the road," Sheena said. "It's got blood on it!"

It was dried and brownish but probably blood, Kate decided, and took the uprooted weed from them.

"Where did you find this?"

"C'mon," said Sheena. "We'll show you."

"No," Kate said decisively. "We'll wait for the sheriff. You all get back in the car. We mustn't touch another thing to disturb this place!"

"Scene of the crime," said Sheena knowingly.

Kate threw her a shut-up look. Edie had her back to them, looking out the car window at the trailer. Kate knew she must be crying. In any case she didn't need to hear any comments from little girls about the hideous thing that must have happened to her neighbor, friend... lover?

For the first time Kate thought of the handsome young man with the white teeth and the crooked smile who had persuaded her to come to these mountains as the person whose blood washed over that room.

Had he been murdered? If not, whose blood was that? Why his absence from the trailer he called home?

The sheriff's office and jail were in a new building back of the pretty little courthouse in Rising Fawn— miles away over tortuous mountain roads—but it did not take Sheriff Jeff Atkins and his single deputy, who followed him, blue lights whirling, long to get there. They pulled up at the edge of the clearing but did not drive into the yard, careful not to obliterate any important tire marks. The sheriff was a young man, new in his job and very polite. He took off his baseball cap and bowed courteously to the women and children as he approached the Blazer.

"You called, Miss Edie?"

Edie wiped her eyes and blew her nose and nodded toward the trailer. "I think somebody has killed Turn. You look... blood everywhere."

"The body...?" began the sheriff.

Kate shook her head. They hadn't looked. There were probably two bedrooms and a bathroom and even closets they could have searched, but they hadn't.

"We didn't go beyond the living room, Sheriff," she said. "Except Edie did use the phone in the kitchen to call you. From the amount of blood it didn't seem likely anybody could have been alive in there, but maybe we should have looked."

"You did right, lady," the young sheriff said, putting on his cap and turning to the trailer. He went in. His deputy waited at the doorsteps. When he emerged, he looked as pale and shaken as Edie and, Kate presumed, she herself had looked. She had seen murder scenes in her time, but nothing to compare with this.

Deputy Byron King, belatedly introduced by Edie, who had grown up with him, looked over Turn's red truck and then accepted the bloody weed, which Kate had left on the hood of the Blazer. He asked the little girls to show him where they found it. Sheena and Kim Sue jumped out with alacrity and led them all, Kate and Edie following, to a spot where a footpath diverged into the woods.

A few yards into the path they found the gravelly soil scuffed up and blood on the ground and on bushes along the path.

"Good God!" said Deputy King. "He must have got away and run this far!"

Edie was sobbing now. "Losing all that blood . . . his leg hurting! Oh, I can't stand it!"

The sheriff took off his cap again and waited a moment for Edie to regain control of herself. Then he asked her very gently to move her car back to the big road while he and his assistant stretched yellow tape around the house and yard.

"Now," he said, looking uncertain but, with almost a boyish resolve, putting his cap back on, "I'll call Atlanta

for forensic help and see if I can get together a search party to look for Representative Pickett...or his body."

"The cavers, Jeff," Edie said. "A lot of them are coming to Dade County today for a big ridge walk. If we hurry, we might catch them before they start out. Some may still be at Pearlie's."

"Right," said the sheriff. "They know these mountains better than anybody else and if he is alive, they can get to him and help him. I'll call on them."

Kate couldn't imagine how much time had elapsed since they themselves had left Pearlie's. It felt like a long day already, but the sun wasn't high and her watch showed a few minutes to ten. Too early for her to find anybody in the office on Saturday, but she felt the old pressure, present in all such emergencies, to reach the city desk. She'd better try Shell at home, and somebody should call the Speaker of the House and maybe even the Governor. They had practically made fun of the young representative, but he was one of their own and they would certainly do something. Kate wasn't sure what.

Deputy King was assigned to stay at the scene, keeping a patrol car for mobility and its radio for communication. It would also serve, as he shiveringly found out, to give him shelter against the biting north wind.

Edie agreed to round up all the cavers she could find and get them to the sheriff's office. Now that she had work to do she seemed calmer, and only her little red nose and her swollen eyes showed that she had been crying.

The Gandys were mercifully quiet.

As soon as they reached the city limits, Kate began

looking for a telephone. "I think I'm probably going to need a motel," she said to Edie. "Can you suggest one?"

"Oh, good!" breathed Kim Sue. "Miss Kate, git one with a swimming pool!"

"Dumb-dumb," jibed Sheena. "You feel that cold?"

"I don't know," said Edie doubtfully. "There's some kind of big festival or convention or something in Chattanooga and all the cavers are coming here. I think the people have overflowed to all the motels in the area, even as far as our town. But we'll find something."

"I'm not particular," said Kate. "Anything with a phone."

"And television," Kim Sue tried again.

Edie smiled. "I'll take you to your car and I guess we'd better go to Pearlie's. Smokey and Jim and some of the others might still be there."

There was still a gathering at the community table and Pearlie had acquired a couple of schoolgirls to help in the kitchen. Edie, followed by Kate, stood a moment at the edge of the crowd, seemingly unable to break the news.

Pearlie was the first to notice.

"What's the matter, sugarfoot? You look like somebody's stole your candy."

Suddenly Edie crumpled against Pearlie's ample bosom.

"He's dead, Pearlie! Turn is dead!"

Conversation at the big table ceased. A half dozen men got to their feet and surrounded Edie. The story came tumbling out. One by one the men picked up their jackets and headed for pickup trucks and vans parked at the door.

"Have some coffee, you all," Pearlie offered.

Edie shook her head. "I'm going with the others. Will you tell Kate where to find a phone and a motel?"

"Damn right," said Pearlie. "She can use my phone and I'll check out Mountain View and Big Rock. There might be something nicer close to Chattanooga, but the way the people have been coming in here I expect all the beds are full."

"I'll start with the phone," Kate said, "and I'll take you up on the coffee."

Shell was down at Bobby Jones Golf Course playing, his wife speculated, or maybe just hanging around.

"I had chores for him to do today," Dora Lee reported petulantly. "This is his way of getting out of them."

"This is Kate Mulcay," Kate began.

"Oh, hi, Kate, what's up? What big story you got for the big city editor this morning?"

"I think it's murder. Will you try to get hold of Shell? A legislator named Turn Pickett, and his trailer here near Rising Fawn is covered with blood. A big search party of cavers is heading out and I think I should go with them. But I'm going to need help—another reporter and, of course, a photographer, maybe two. After all, it is a legislator."

"I'll have him paged and if that doesn't get him I'll run down there and look for him," Dora Lee said promptly, now in her role as the well-trained city editor's wife.

"I'll call back as soon as I find a place to stay," Kate said. "Meanwhile, if Shell tries to reach me, tell him to try the office of Sheriff Jeff Atkins in Rising Fawn."

Pearlie, with a portable phone tucked under her dangling blue plastic earring, had made her calls while she turned bacon and flipped hotcakes. They had yielded nothing. The only thing she could suggest was an old-fashioned tourist cabin over near the Tennessee River.

"It ain't the Henry Grady Hotel," Pearlie said, "but it's a roof and a bed."

Kate wanted to tell her that she was glad it wasn't the Henry Grady. That famous old state-owned hostelry, center of the state's political life for generations, had been demolished a decade ago to make room for a gleaming mirrored tower called the Plaza.

"Whatever you find will be all right," she assured Pearlie. "I hope it has a telephone."

"Aw, probably not in the room," said Pearlie. "It ain't that up-to-date. But Addie Armentrout runs it and I know she has a phone in the office. You can use that."

That was discouraging, but Kate thought it would have to do until she could do better. If she had known what she was running into she would have brought a portable computer, but a phone anywhere would serve. She had dictated from phones in all kinds of places, the worst probably from a roadside pay station with a broken-down door and chicken trucks thundering by in a smelly procession. It had been impossible to hear herself, much less anything the rewrite man back at the office had to say.

"Would you give me directions and ask Mrs. Armentrout to hold a cabin for me?" Kate asked. "I need to get to the sheriff's office now, but I'll get to her place later."

Kate walked into the sheriff's office to find eight or ten cavers in their boots and hard hats standing around the sheriff's desk.

"Call came for you, Kate," said Edie. "I think it was your boss. Said call him back."

For once Shell seemed excited over what her colleagues called "one of Kate's murders."

"The Speaker has appointed a special committee of House members to come up there and help with the search, if necessary," Shell said. "He's going to ask the Governor to dispatch the Georgia Bureau of Investigation and it could be he'll alert the civil defense. Now I need a quick story for the Sunday paper. All that you know about this Pickett fellow, circumstances of the killing... you know."

"Until the body is found," Kate said carefully, aware that all the cavers were listening, "we can only assume that it was a killing. I know very little about Representative Pickett now, but I'll get on it and call you back. First deadline for Sunday?"

"You got it," Shell said. He was leaving for the office to mobilize the photographic staff and find a reporter to help out at that end. "Did you get a room? Got a telephone number?"

Kate turned to the caver group. "Anybody know Miss Armentrout's telephone number?"

"Oh, good Lord, is that where you're staying?" asked Edie.

Kate turned back to the phone and told Shell, "I'll get back to you with that number," and hung up.

"Honey, you'd do better if the sheriff here put you in jail," said Smokey.

"I haven't seen the place," Kate admitted. "But Miss Pearlie said it was the only thing left. I haven't any time to look. I have to call the office back with something on Mr. Pickett. What can you all tell me?"

One of them looked up the number of the tourist court, which was called "Home in the Pines"—formerly, one young man said with a leer, the "No Tell Inn."

"I don't care about its sordid past," Kate said. "I just need a place for the night. Now about Mr. Pickett."

They were willing to cooperate, but they really didn't know much. They thought he was about thirty years old. He had come to Georgia from the Indian reservation in Oklahoma or somewhere out there. Nobody was sure where. He attended Georgia Tech and after graduation came to find a place in the mountains. He immediately claimed Rising Fawn for his home, bought a trailer from a coal mining family that was moving, and established residency.

"Work?" said Kate, scribbling in a notebook.

"He was an engineer," said Edie. "Worked some with the highway department and left there to work with the Forest Service. I think he liked that best of all."

"A good caver," put in somebody else. "Jim taught him to rappel a while back and he spent a lot of weekends doing that. Hurt himself saving a young girl who didn't know what she was doing and got out of control on

Pigeon Mountain. Liked to be by himself a lot and surprised us all by getting enough votes to be elected to the legislature. He ran on the platform of getting Georgia land back from Tennessee."

The man laughed. "We're all for that."

"Family?" asked Kate.

They all looked at Edie.

"He spoke of family," she said, flushing a little. "I think he meant tribal family. He said his parents are dead. I don't know any names or addresses."

"I was gon' ask you, Edie," said the sheriff, coming to his door. "Do you know his next of kin?"

Edie shook her head miserably.

"We got to notify somebody," the sheriff said.

"Have you asked at the post office?" asked Kate. "He must have received and sent mail. And the Forest Service? Doesn't the state require a lot of vital statistics when they hire somebody?"

"Good idea, ma'am," said the sheriff. "This is my first case like this and I appreciate all the help I can get."

"Share and share alike," said Kate, smiling at him. "I've got to dictate a story pretty soon and facts like that will be important."

The cavers were still there and directionless when Jim arrived. A wave of relief seemed to pass over the group, washing over the young sheriff. He thrust out a hand, although he had probably seen and spoken to Jim already that day.

"Man, I'm glad to see you!" he said unabashedly. "I

didn't know where to tell them to start. I know you know how to look for a person, dead or alive."

"We can try," said Jim gravely. "I'm sorry it's Turn."

"Well, I leave it to you all. Just be careful of anything that might be evidence. You know, tracks, people, or vehicles. We'll make the Blue Hole the . . . what's the term for it?"

"Meeting place," said Jim, grinning.

"Yeah, meeting place," said the sheriff, relieved that it was something so simple and untechnical.

The cavers filed out and climbed into two four-wheel-drive trucks at the curb. Edie collected a hard hat, a flashlight, a coil of rope, and some other gear from her car and climbed in with them. The sheriff, busy on the phone to the post office, motioned Kate and the Gandy girls into his office.

"You can have this phone in a minute, Mrs. Mulcay," the sheriff said. "As soon as I get an affirmative from the state crime lab and the GBI, I'll be out in the field with the search party. Take my chair and if you need a typewriter . . . " He waved to one on a stand by the window.

His eyes fell on Sheena and Kim Sue.

"Young ladies, you want a Coke? Here, be my guest!" He pulled some coins out of his pocket and pointed to the drink stand in the outer office.

Kate had almost forgotten the girls and now she damned their irresponsible mother for parking them on her without so much as a by-your-leave. They had relatives by the dozen. Young Mrs. Gandy didn't seem to realize that when Kate had to work, she didn't need two little girls along. But then—Kate's better nature surfaced—she hadn't known she was going to have to work and the girls, thinking of Rock City, might have overpersuaded their mother.

The sheriff hung up the phone and reached for his jacket. "They're sending a helicopter from Atlanta," he said. He patted his belt, which held a beeper in addition to such other gear as a pistol and a flashlight. "My girl is off today, but I've called her to come in special and she'll call me if need be. Name's Lorena."

He got to the door and turned back. "Mrs. Harbin at the post office said the only mail Turn ever got was from around here. If he heard from anybody out West she didn't know it. Forest Service had the shortest kind of bio. They needed rangers and he had been to Tech and was a minority besides."

"Oh, yes," said Kate. "Cherokee. That would give him some kind of priority, I suppose. And Tech is bound to have something on his application and at least whatever they put in the yearbook."

She dialed Shell.

"Get somebody to check Georgia Tech and the Department of Transportation. He also worked for the Forest Service and they must have something in their personnel files. The clerk's office in the House of Representatives will at least have a short bio. If you can't find anybody in on Saturday, try the clerk at home. Wait, I have his number." She fumbled in her bag and brought out an address book and read the clerk's number to Shell, who wrote it down and hung up.

The sheriff got as far as the outside door, where he met a tall, doleful-looking woman with blue-black hair piled in an intricate arrangement on top of her head and deep shadows under her eyes. She was divesting herself of a handsome fur coat.

"Mrs. Mulcay, this is Lorena," the sheriff called over his shoulder. "She runs the office. Lorena, help Mrs. Mulcay any way you can. She's from the *Atlanta Searchlight*."

Kate stood up from the sheriff's desk chair and extended a hand.

"I'm Kate. Glad to meet you."

Lorena nodded, noncommittal. She put her coat in a cleaner's bag, which hung from a rack on the office wall.

"These your children?" she asked, looking disapprovingly at Sheena and Kim Sue, who occupied the one big rocker in the room, sucking away on Coke cans.

"Neighbors," said Kate. "Sheena and Kim Sue Gandy. We were just coming up here for a look at the mountains—nice weekend trip—when all this happened and I had to get to work."

"Was going to see Rock City," said Kim Sue dolefully.

"Well, it ain't all that great," said Lorena. "Say you can see seven states from up there, but I never have. You can put your foot, your own foot, on three states here in Dade County."

"Oooh!" gasped the girls together. "Miss Kate, can we—"

Kate shook her head. "Not now." She returned to her

notes. In a few minutes she was ready to dictate a story to a hastily conscripted rewrite man.

"Here's the place for his background," she directed after she had dictated a few paragraphs. "Shell has some-body checking that. And then develop that part about his effort to get the legislature to study the Georgia-Tennessee line and act to reclaim a chunk of mountain, which he said was stolen from his Cherokee ancestors. His grandfather was the famous Cherokee war chief named Dragging Canoe."

"Are you kidding?" The rewrite man laughed. "Nobody ever had a name like that, Cherokee or not."

"Wanta bet?" said Kate. "You ever hear of Going Snake or Hanging Maw?"

"My God, it gets worse," muttered the rewrite man.

"Or better," said Kate. "Depends on how you feel about Native Americans. I like them to have colorful names. Oh, be sure to add a line that Representative Pickett's resolution was recommitted to the House State Institutions and Property Committee for further study. The chairman of that committee is Representative Tol-bert Keys of Waycross. Tell Shell. Somebody ought to call him for comment."

Before the rewrite man checked his computer for spelling and released Kate, Shell came on the line.

"We've called that statesman in south Georgia. Half the committee is on the way to Rising Fawn in a state helicopter."

Poor old Turn, thought Kate, turning from the phone when the call was ended. *Not much attention in life. But*

51

now that they think he's dead they're going all-out.

She collected hers and the little girls' jackets from the rack where Lorena's fur coat hung encased in plastic.

"Pretty coat," she said to make conversation with the melancholy woman who sat at a desk in the corner, her elbows on a typewriter she hadn't uncovered yet.

Kate didn't really like furs herself, but she recognized that, as furs went, this one was excellent. How did this plain gaunt woman clerk in an office in the smallest county in the state afford such opulence?

"I hate it," said Lorena surprisingly. "It's what men give you when they leave you."

"Oh," said Kate weakly. She supposed she had been left a time or two in her life before that endurer, Benjy, had stayed the course. But nobody ever gave her a fur coat. "You ought to write a song about it," she told Lorena. It might not make Broadway, but it seemed a natural for Nashville.

Back in the car she realized she had not asked directions for the motel or the cavers' meeting place, the Blue Hole. They shouldn't be hard to find.

First for the "Home in the Pines" to cinch a room for the night. The road climbed and instead of the altitude bringing them closer to the sun, the great brassy globe they had seen from the valley disappeared and rain was falling.

"Look for a lot of pine trees, girls," she said. "And a sign that says 'Home in the Pines.' That will be our home for the night."

"Will there be a swimming pool?" Kim Sue asked.

Kate threw her a derisive look and Sheena gave her the brutal truth. "Neither that or teevee, either, I bet."

"Aw, shi...OOT!" said Kim Sue, correcting herself.

Kate sighed. "Look," she said, "this is not going to be one of those fun days. We're going to see if we can help the sheriff and all those other people find a poor man who may be lost in the mountains, badly hurt. I'd hate to think that you were the kind of girls who worried about things for your own pleasure when you could be helping somebody else."

Even as she talked, she knew that Turn Pickett's body would be what they found and she didn't want the children to see that. She couldn't get their mother to come and take them off her hands because even if the BMW ran—and it had been practically totaled twice when their father, as the family put it, "took on a little too much"— young Mrs. Gandy was doing bedside service for her baby-having sister.

I'll think of something, Kate promised herself even as a battered sign with air rifle holes pockmarking it in rust appeared. The marksman must have been trying to hit the "I" in PINES, Kate thought. That would have only been sporting.

She turned in on an unpaved, pine-needle-carpeted driveway to a vibrantly blue hut with a sagging sign which said OFFICE. She knocked on the door and a strident voice called out, "Hell-o, babee!" Startled, Kate stepped back involuntarily as the girls yelled, "Here she comes, Miss Kate! Here the lady comes!"

Kate wasn't sure "lady" was the term she would have

applied to the enormously fat woman in a flowered shift, a World War II Army jacket, and rubber waders used for trout fishing. But she had to appreciate her cordiality.

"Why, Kate Mulcay!" cried Addie Armentrout. "I'm as tickled as a jaybird in whistling time to meet you! I read your colyum just about every time I git my hands on the Atlanta paper. You all charging so high," she said in a confidential whisper, "I mostly have to wait for one of my guests to leave one behind."

"Ah, that's nice of you," said Kate. "I appreciate your going to that trouble. Did Pearlie at the restaurant call about my little girls and me?"

"Good God, yes!" cried the lady, just as the voice in the office shrieked "Hell-o, babee!" again. She smiled proudly in that direction. "My mynah bird." And then she went on in her businesslike tone, "She didn't mention no young'uns. Does your'n wet the bed?"

"Not in years," said Kate, smiling.

"Well, I reckon I can let you have a rollaway—five dollars extry. How's that?"

"Maybe I should see the cabin first," said Kate doubtfully, her eyes on the row of sagging little shacks, one painted silver and the others in pastel rose, blue, and yellow, with one a deep pulsing purple.

Sheena and Kim Sue were already out of the car walking toward them. Children of the Holiday Inn age, what were they likely to say of this remnant of Model-T Fords and dirt roads? Surprisingly, they were ecstatic.

"Looka yonder, Miss Kate, they're dollhouses!" caroled Sheena.

The mynah bird shrilled "Hell-o-o, babee!" and the girls were stopped in their tracks, big-eyed and excited. They rushed back to the office and peered through the window.

"Oooh!" they squealed together. "You're the purtiest thing!"

Mrs. Armentrout looked very proud. "I got a baby bear, too," she whispered. "Don't tell nobody. Them governmints would take it—or me one. Say it's agin the law, but feller who rented from me were a hunter and he killed its ma. So tenderhearted he brought me the cub. I keep it back yonder in the woods so nobody will see it and report me. But you girls . . . if you're quiet-like and gentle, I reckon you could play with it some."

The excitement and appeal on the freckled faces was too much, Kate thought. "We gon' stay, ain't we?" asked Sheena. Mindful of the fact that there were no other accommodations within miles, Kate relented.

"Sure," she said. Whatever the condition of the cabin short of downright filth and squalor, she supposed it was theirs for one night, at least.

"The silver one, the silver one!" chanted Sheena, pulling herself away from the window and the mynah bird.

"No, purple, purple!" shouted Kim Sue.

"No, not purple," Kate said decisively. She didn't want to explain that she hated purple in all things except lilacs and violets and iris and wisteria. She just didn't feel lucky or secure enough to face sleeping enveloped in purple.

"Silver, then," said Sheena triumphantly.

"It is the closest to the office and the telephone Pearlie said you'd want to use," said Mrs. Armentrout, justifying the choice. "They're all nice," she added modestly. "I kinda like silver myself. I was thinking about maybe painting them all silver and renaming my place the Silver Comet."

"Nice," said Kate feebly, thinking the cabin she approached looked like the radiator grill on a 1938 Buick.

The interior was surprisingly fresh and clean. The one window was open to the cold outside air and the rain. Mrs. Armentrout pulled it down.

"Had a drunk last week," she explained. "Takes a time to air out the stink."

But the double bed under a chenille spread with a flamboyant peacock worked in a dozen bright colors looked clean. The little dresser was topped by a plastic scarf with ruffles on it. There was a bathroom, shower instead of tub, and except for the inevitable rust stains, it appeared to have been well scrubbed. Linoleum covered the floor and a small potbellied stove, anchored in a box of sand, occupied one wall.

"Wood outside," said Mrs. Armentrout. "I reckon you know how to build a fire if you need it."

"If you'll let us have a rollaway bed," Kate said, "we can manage fine here. Now can we see the baby bear?"

"I'm gon' take you there right soon," said the proprietor. "But first, wouldn't you like to sample one of my fried peach pies? I made 'em this morning because my grand-young'uns usually come stay with me on Saturday. You all will like them. Boy and a girl. He's the oldest, named Kevin, fourteen years old. She's Debbie, about your age," looking at Sheena. "Prettiest yeller curly hair."

Kate could see interest in the fourteen-year-old boy sparking between age twelve and eleven. "Hurry and see the bear, girls," she said, "and ask Mrs. Armentrout to let you take the fried pies with you. I've got to hurry to the Blue Hole and see what the search party is doing."

"They could stay here with me," Mrs. Armentrout offered. "My grandkids would be tickled to death to have company and there's lots to see. We even got a little cave in the back where they can make a playhouse."

"Oh, may I see that?" asked Kate. "If I'm going to leave them with you . . . "

The cave was a shallow scoop at the base of the mountain, the kind country people in the days before electric freezers stored their winter fruits and vegetables in. It had a heavy door and a clean white sand floor with no dark corners. It seemed safe enough, but Kate hesitated. This comfortable, hospitable woman was, after all, a stranger.

"Oh, please, Miss Kate, let us stay," begged Sheena. "Please!"

"Please!" echoed Kim Sue.

The alternative, Kate thought, was taking them into the wilds of Scratch Ankle where a body might be found—no suitable Saturday outing for little girls.

"Well, I guess it will be all right," she said slowly. "And it's very nice of Mrs. Armentrout to invite you."

"You can pay me now," said Mrs. Armentrout briskly.

"Advance is when it's due—twenty-five dollars for the cabin and five for the rollaway bed. I throw in the baby-sitting."

That was a false note in the great wash of hospitality, Kate thought as she handed over $30. But the woman was right. She would be baby-sitting.

"I'll get back as soon as I can. And I may bring some more people with me, photographers from the paper and maybe some legislators, if they haven't managed reservations in Chattanooga or with friends."

"Anything, anybody," said Mrs. Armentrout. "I've got four more vacancies."

Kate got directions to the Blue Hole and drove out, with the little girls waving happily and heading for the wooded area back of the cluster of cabins, where presumably the offspring of Smokey the Bear awaited them.

The Blue Hole was the prettiest little stream Kate thought she had ever seen, sapphire water which seemed to be flowing from a rock on the side of the mountain. Kate couldn't see its source—no waterfall, no cascading stream, simply bright blue water cupped in a little rocky pool and flowing jauntily into a grassy field, where the state helicopter and four legislators had already landed.

Kate walked toward them. She recognized a couple of them, one an old-timer who once had run for lieutenant governor—unsuccessfully—and a bumptious young fellow from one of the twenty counties in the metropolitan Atlanta area. They waved and seemed on the verge of greeting her gaily until they apparently remembered the gravity of their mission, the disappearance and possible death of one of their number, a young man who had now taken on the aura of sterling character and incalculable value to their state.

The two she knew greeted Kate with more cordiality than she thought their acquaintance warranted—Representative Cecil Hawkins from the tobacco belt in south Georgia and Representative Motley Banks from urban Gwinnett County. They introduced Representative Harry Hinson, who came from neighboring Walker County just across the line from Dade, and Representative Trent Goodman, who had the good fortune to be from the peach- and cotton-growing area where the celebrated U.S. Senator Walter George had lived. Georgia politicians enjoyed invoking the name of the late senator because he had made history during the Roosevelt administration by opposing the president's effort to expand the U.S. Supreme Court and then dealing a smashing defeat to the man the president chose to take Senator George's place in the Senate. Even people who liked Mr. Roosevelt rejoiced in the old senator's defiance and his triumph.

Goodman was a handsome, white-haired man with a heavy, well-fleshed body and a voice that rang out independent of microphones when he chose to speak in the House. His speech had an excessively fulsome flavor even in ordinary conversation.

Now he grabbed both of Kate's hands and looked deeply into her eyes, intoning sonorously, "Mrs. Mulcay, you know what a grievous thing this is! You understand our travail! We are here to do everything in the Georgia General Assembly's power to find that young man and to vindicate the heinous crime that has been done to him!"

Kate wanted to say *I'm not ready to quote you yet, Representative,* but the young fellow from the county next door was getting in his licks: "You better believe we gon' vindicate! Turn was fighting for our Georgia land and I, for one, am gon' see that he did not . . . "—he started to say *die in vain,* Kate thought, but he quickly changed course—"didn't fight in vain. I'm on the State Institutions and Property Committee and I glory in the responsibility we carry to be vigilant about the state's property."

He pointed toward the mountain, but Kate had a feeling that he wasn't sure of his directions. It was very confusing, this end of the ninety-mile-long Lookout Mountain and its neighbor, Sand Mountain. She was far from figuring out north and south, and as for the famed Rock City the girls yearned to see and the more famous Chickamauga battlefield, which she would like to see, she would have to get a map to find them.

The other two members of the delegation were busy hauling overnight bags and briefcases out of the helicopter and did not commit themselves.

"We couldn't make a hotel reservation," Representative Banks said. "But that's all right, we're rugged fellows, aren't we, boys? I brought along some camping equipment. A tent and a stove and some sleeping bags. You know a good camp spot?"

Kate had seen charred remnants of an old campfire across the little creek flowing from the Blue Hole. She pointed it out.

"This is supposed to be the meeting place of the cavers who are doing the searching," she said. "I'm expecting one of our photographers to meet me here. There is a kind of primitive motel about five miles from here. I got a room and the proprietor said she had four vacancies available when I left. But this may be handier for the search."

The portly Representative Goodman looked at the falling rain, laced with sleet. Clearly not an outdoorsman, he said, "Where did you say that motel is?"

"I can go home," said Representative Hinson, who was a Chickamauga real estate salesman. "I live only about twenty miles from here. I've asked them"—he nodded toward his colleagues—"but they want to stay on the ground."

Kate rested her eyes on the magical Blue Hole and the towering rocks above it. The little creek flowing from it was glazed with ice around the edges, but when they got the tent up and a fire built, it might beat the multicolored cabins by a mile. The luxury-loving girls might even be charmed by it, although Kate, an old camper herself, couldn't be sure about that.

At that moment she saw a red-clad figure swinging by a rope halfway down the mountainside. She went closer and the figure landed.

It was Edie.

A sharp intake of breath, and Kate went closer. "You could have fallen!"

"Sure," said the schoolteacher, grinning. "You can do that, all right. But I had good instruction. Jim. And I've done it lots of times. I came down to start some hot coffee and food arrangements for the rest of them. They still haven't found any trace of Turn."

She divested herself of rappelling gear. "Where are the girls?"

"Oh, I abandoned those brats," said Kate flippantly. And then seriously, "I left them with that nice Mrs. Armentrout. She was gon' give them fried pies and let them play with her bear cub and grandson and -daughter."

Edie dropped a rope and took a deep breath.

"Kate," she said urgently, "Addie Armentrout does not have any grandchildren. And that bear cub she had grew up and returned to the wild ten or fifteen years ago! Kate, we'd better—"

But Kate was running for her car.

CHAPTER TWO

AS KATE REACHED her car, Representative Hinson saw her from across the creek and came running, teetering precariously on the footlog that crossed the creek. "What's the trouble? Can I help?"

"No...yes! I don't know," cried Kate. "Two little girls I brought with me.... I left them with a woman.... She may be crazy. I've got to go!"

"I'll go with you," Hinson cried, jumping in the passenger seat.

Edie was wresting open the back door even as the car moved toward the highway.

"Where is this place?" asked Hinson.

"Oh, I hope I can remember...." muttered Kate through clenched teeth.

"I know," said Edie. "Scratch Ankle Road. I don't know why Pearlie sent you there. The woman is crazy."

"The place was clean," babbled Kate, "and fried pies..."

"Yes," said Edie. "It may be all right. She hasn't hurt anybody that I ever heard of and the motel brings her a living. But she is crazy. It's best that we go and see."

Kate was holding back tears. A sob caught in her throat and she said chokily, "I shouldn't . . . I shouldn't have left them."

"It's probably all right," said Edie. "She's a strange old thing, but I don't know that there's any harm in her. That about the grandchildren and the cub . . . that worries me a little. And her family has always lived on Scratch Ankle Road."

"What does that mean?" asked Hinson.

"Coal miners," said Edie. "Going back to the days when the owners leased convict labor and made them work in chains and shackles. You can see signs on the rocks where they dragged their chains."

"Oh, dear God!" cried Kate. "Generations of anger and hostility and grudges."

"Maybe not," said Edie. "I'm not sure that her granddaddy was one of those they starved and beat."

"Oh, dear God!" cried Kate again, and tromped down on the accelerator.

The little tourist court seemed peaceful—too peaceful. The door to the office was locked and so were the multicolored cabins. Kate ran from one to the other, trying the doors. Edie, standing on tiptoe to peer in the office window, saw no movement and heard no sound but the mynah bird's jubilant "Hell-o, babee!" when it realized it had an audience.

Kate ran toward the woods, calling the girls' names.

64

Edie and Hinson searched the driveway for footprints, but the rain had begun to fall harder and there was scant chance of any recognizable tracks in the gravelly soil.

Kate turned to Edie and Hinson, rigid with fear. "The sheriff..." she said, "I want to call the sheriff."

"Yes," said Edie, "the sheriff." And she picked up a rock and sent it through a pane of glass in the office door.

"Good shot," approbated Kate, poking her hand though the jagged glass and fumbling for the door lock.

"I don't know. Should you have done that?" protested Representative Hinson weakly.

"Damned right she should have," said Kate, searching for the door lock. Her hand refused to find it, but by stretching she could barely reach an old-fashioned black telephone.

She pulled it through the broken window and dialed 911. An answer was a long time coming. Perhaps everybody was out on the mountain search for Return Pickett. After a long spate of futile ringing, Lorena answered in a dull and listless voice. She said she would try to get the sheriff on the radio or on his beeper.

"Please hurry," begged Kate. "There's no sign of my girls or of that Mrs. Armentrout and I'm worried."

"Addie Armentrout?" asked Lorena. "Good God a'mighty! I'll git somebody there right away—or come myself."

Lorena's reaction was alarming. What did she know about Addie Armentrout? As for coming herself, Kate had little hope that Lorena in her consolation fur coat would be of much help, but she welcomed anybody. The way the wind had risen and the rain was whipping across the valley, she almost wished for the fur coat herself.

The three of them huddled under the only big pine tree in the yard. It was meager protection, but they couldn't bring themselves to leave the front of the office for the shelter of the car. Maybe the phone would ring or maybe Addie and the girls would emerge from the Scratch Ankle undergrowth.

The sheriff arrived faster than Kate had hoped.

"I was at Turn's trailer with the guys from the state crime lab," he explained. "What's this about Addie Armentrout killing some young'uns?"

Kate turned pale and grabbed hold of Edie and Hinson to keep from falling. "Killed?" she stammered.

The young sheriff's face went blank. "I thought Lorena said . . . Well, what is the problem?"

"Sheriff, the woman and the little girls have simply disappeared," put in Representative Hinson. "Kate is worried because apparently the woman told her some tall tales and she is afraid that the woman might be . . . well, deranged."

"Well, yeah, she *is* that," said the sheriff. "Nuts. Whole family was. But I don't know if she would harm anybody."

"Kidnap," said Kate weakly. "Would she try to kidnap them?"

Edie closed her eyes and opened them in shock and disbelief, as if, Kate thought, she believed it had happened.

"You think she would?" Kate said.

"No, no, I don't know," said Edie. "But you know women who are crazy about kids and never had any . . . I just thought the way Addie was making up those fictitious grandchildren."

The sheriff interrupted the grim imagining. "Let me call for some help and start looking," he said. "Edie, Harry, you want to stay or come with me?"

"Okay to leave you?" Edie asked, and Kate nodded. Whatever they could do to find the children was what was important. She dared not leave.

Representative Hinson said he would hitch a ride with the sheriff back to the Blue Hole and enlist the help of the other legislators. They were probably only waiting there for some direction from the cavers, and the sheriff might put them to work.

The three of them got in the sheriff's car, but then Edie jumped out and ran toward Kate, pulling off her down vest.

"Here, I've got another jacket in my car. This will keep you a little warmer."

Kate slipped the vest on under her own jacket, grateful for its warmth, and sat down on the single step to the little office. Oh, those children would be cold, wherever they were. She remembered reading that Anne Lindbergh, distraught over the disappearance of her little baby, worried a lot that he had been taken with nothing on but his sleepers and he might be cold. It was a small consideration. If only they were safe, she wouldn't worry that they might be a little sick. You could treat colds and croup, but suppose they never came back . . . suppose they were dead? She thought she ought to call their mother, but perhaps it was pointless to get her upset and frightened so soon. She looked at her watch. It had been only a couple of hours since the girls had waved her a cheery good-bye and gone toward the woods to see the baby bear.

That bear . . . She stood up. Edie said it had been years since Addie's bear was a cub. It had grown up and now eluded hunters in the dense woods along the mountaintop. But suppose the girls went looking and got lost back there? Suppose there really was a cub and its mother attacked them?

She took the path around the cluster of cabins to the woods beyond. She passed the cave and noticed that its big timbered door was closed. She went on by means of awkward handholds and slipping feet, clutching at big rocks and using her knees when her feet skidded out from under her. Vicious briars tore at her clothes and the rain made the great sandstone rocks slippery. Her hands and her knees, striving for purchase, were skinned and bloody.

A slender cedar tree grew out of a cleft in the rock and Kate grabbed for its trunk to hoist herself up.

It was then she heard voices—young girl voices!

"Sheena! Kim Sue!" she shouted. "Where are you?"

There was no answer, and then there was a faint "Here, Miss Kate, in a hole in the ground!"

"Oh, thank God!" Kate breathed. "Are you all right? Can you get out?"

"We all right," faltered Kim Sue, "but we cain't find

no way out of this hole. Rocks keep a-falling and penning us up."

Their voices seemed to come from a big rock right in front of Kate. There was, in truth, no opening.

"Be still. Be very still," said Kate. "If you wiggle around, you might dislodge a big rock, and that would make it harder for us to get you out." But displaying more optimism than she felt, she added, "We're going to get you out—and soon!"

"There was this rock we stepped on," said Sheena. "We was just climbing looking for a way out—and it fell!" Her voice broke and Kate thought, *Not Sheena crying; she never cries! Poor babies, poor scared meddlesome young'uns!*

"You stay put," she said, "and I'll run and find somebody who knows about caves and can get you out without any trouble."

"Miss Kate, don't leave us," pleaded Kim Sue, and Kate thought she might cry. "Oh, honey, I'll be right back with someone who can get you out," she said. "Don't worry."

She didn't notice the brambles or the rocks on the way down. She simply sat down and slid halfway, and when sliding was impossible she found a tree branch and swung over a big crevass she hadn't noticed on the way up.

There was a car in the yard when Kate got there. In it were Lorena and the big man called PawPaw, and emerging from the motel office was...Addie Armentrout!

The sheriff arrived as Kate, ready to throttle her, reached Addie's side.

"Do you know what you did to my little girls?" she shouted. "They're trapped in a cave!"

"What's that?" said the sheriff. "You've found the children?"

Kate pointed wordlessly to the cave. The sheriff strode to the barred door in the side of the hill, with Kate at his heels and PawPaw close behind them. Lorena stayed behind with Addie, who was humming as she unwrapped birdseed for her mynah bird.

With the bar lifted and the big door open, the cave was fairly light, and the sheriff, training his flashlight upward, saw that two rocks had been dislodged—the first one apparently by the girls themselves, who moved it to investigate the possibility of an exit. It had fallen back in place, jarring loose a second one, which effectively trapped them.

The sheriff turned helplessly to PawPaw. "I'm no caver, but I'm willing to go up there and try to pull those rocks out."

"I know how to do it," said PawPaw, but, looking down at his substantial girth, he added, "I don't believe I can fit in that shaft."

"I can," said Kate. "I'll go up there. Just tell me what to do."

The men were peering at the jagged chunk of sandstone that the girls had dislodged.

"The danger," said PawPaw, "is that you might set off an avalanche when you start pulling at that first rock. We don't know if it's loose. Let me go find Jim and Smokey."

"Hey, girls," called Kate, "can you hear us? We'll be getting you out soon."

"Yes'm," said one of them meekly.

Oh, Lord, thought Kate, *now they are getting meek. They must really be scared.* And the early winter twilight was falling. *Suppose we can't get them out before dark?*

"Sheriff," she said in a panic, "it's getting dark!"

"Don't worry, honey," he said, unexpectedly putting his arm around her shoulders. "We got floodlights on the way. Also, Jim and Smokey have been notified and they'll be here any minute. They are our best cavers, always know what to do in a tight situation."

Kate took up a post inside the shallow cave where the children thought they were going to have a playhouse. Seated on the ground, she looked upward at the impenetrable ceiling and talked to them. The answers were mumbled and barely distinct, but she talked anyway, wanting to ask questions but making herself shout reassurances instead.

The rescue truck from the fire department whirled up and presently the hillside was illuminated like a stage. Somebody built a fire between the office and the mouth of the cave, and Mrs. Armentrout, followed by Lorena, moved close to warm herself.

"What are these people doing in my yard?" she demanded. "Might be ruining my business."

Kate dared not speak to her, but the sheriff did. "Lorena says she found you shopping at Wal-Mart when she went out on her break. Why did you shut those little girls up in the cave?"

"Would you take young'uns to the Wal-Mart?" she countered irritably. "Biggest pest in the world, young'uns, when you want to do your trading. I had to git a cuttle-bone for my mynah bird, so I told them to play nice till I got back."

"But you shut that door and put the bar on it," pointed out the sheriff. "They couldn't get out that way and so they tried to climb to the top. That's where they are now and they are trapped, Addie. You know, you have committed a crime."

"I declare," murmured Addie with mild interest, turning her backside to the fire and hoisting her flowered skirt.

Kate wanted to say, *You old monster. You lied to them and you have terrified them and endangered their lives.* But she felt so much blame on herself for leaving them with a stranger and she thought it might be an exaggeration to say the Gandys were terrified. Inconvenienced, yes. Endangered and disappointed, of course. With dark settling on the mountain they would be cold and scared, but not terrified. The sturdy, self-possessed young Gandys didn't terrify easily.

All thought of the missing Return Pickett had slipped from Kate's mind. She wondered impatiently where those premier cavers, Jim and Smokey, were.

Suddenly they were there in their hard hats and boots, exuding confidence. They nodded to her and went directly to the sheriff.

"No trace of Turn," said Smokey.

"What do we have here?" asked Jim.

"It's Addie's cave," explained the sheriff. "She locked the two little girls in it and went to town. They must

72

have seen a rock in the ceiling that they thought they could move. It's one of those chimney-shaped caves, you know. They pushed the rock aside and started climbing and I reckon it fell back in place, shutting them off from the bottom and then another one fell. Sounds like they are near the top but there's a big rock there and we are fearful of trying to move it. What do you think?"

The two men climbed the mountainside the way Kate had but were more surefooted and nimble. At the top Kate heard them talking to the girls. Were they getting plenty of air? Could they see light? Air blew in from somewhere but it was very dark.

"I think we'll move this one, fellers," Jim called down the hill. "Need muscle, you all. Come on up but take it easy and slow."

The sheriff and PawPaw and two men from the fire truck obeyed. Jim deployed them around the great sandstone "floater," a boulder which was not anchored in the earth. "Grab the come-along. It's in the jeep," he directed Kate.

In her haste to do something constructive Kate stumbled, scrambled to her feet and stumbled again. Smokey met her halfway down the slope and took the tool from her hands.

Jim was busy tying a rope around the boulder. If it fell, she thought anxiously, it might jar loose more rocks inside the cave. It might even crush the girls who waited on the other side.

Oh, God, let it work, she prayed soundlessly. *Let them out.*

The idea, Jim told his helpers, was not to try to lift the rock, but to ease it off to one side, shifting it away from the opening to the cave. He and Smokey manned the ropes. The others laid hands on the boulder and waited for the signal.

"All together, now," said Jim. "Push! Push!"

"Heave ho!" shouted Addie from her place by the fire.

"Shut up," muttered Kate between clenched teeth.

The giant "floater," which had not floated in a couple of thousand years, did not float now, but there was a barely perceptible movement.

"Again," said Smokey, pumping the come-along. "All together...*push!*"

An inch or two at a time, agonizingly, slowly, they edged the monster from its resting place. Once in a while they caught their breath. Jim used the pick to clear a path for the big rock, pulling away smaller rocks and bushes.

"Now again!" he cried, and they pushed.

Suddenly there was sound from the shaft.

"We see light!" yelled Sheena.

"Kin we git out now?" importuned Kim Sue.

"Not yet," said Jim. "Not quite yet. Be very still and we'll have you on the ground in no time." He eased his hand into the little aperture that moving the rock had opened up, to make sure there were no other rocks that might turn loose from the cave wall and further trap the girls.

At that moment a wrecker with its roof light blazing

pulled up in the yard. The sheriff's call for help had been heard. The driver got out and strode to the foot of the mountain.

"I got a cable and a hoist, Jim. Want 'em?"

"Can you reach this far?" asked Jim. "Give it a try, Bud. Be easy backing up."

Bud nodded and returned to the wrecker, backing it slowly over the rough grass and bushes and rocks that edged the little path to the cave. Suddenly there was a roar on the road and a big yellow piece of earth-moving machinery appeared.

The young volunteer firemen, blowing on their cold, skinned hands, smiled broadly.

"Hot damn!" said one. "A bulldozer!"

Edie, wearing a jumpsuit and a fleece-lined denim jacket, jumped out of the bulldozer cab and ran across the yard. "More coming," she said. "Trucks with chains and shovels. Lot of manpower from Pearlie's. Ambulance, just in case."

Kate watched the procession of vehicles on the little dirt road and choked back tears. "Bless them! Bless them!" she murmured. "So many of them coming to help!"

"The legislators aren't coming," Edie told them. "They still haven't found Turn, and that big talky man who was with them—Representative Banks, I think—is also missing. He was with them when they started checking Running Water Creek and then he wasn't."

"How long ago?" asked Kate.

"About noon, I think. Just after we came over here."

Suddenly the big boulder, like a sleeping animal, seemed to breathe . . . and stir.

"Rock! Look out below!" shouted Jim. He and Smokey tried to hold back on the ropes, but the ropes snapped and the big boulder began to move. "Get outa the way, Bud!" Jim hollered at the wrecker driver. "Run, evvabody!"

Everybody did run, and the wrecker, which fortunately still had its motor going, skidded across the yard just in time. Kate couldn't be sure what had happened. She was scrambling up the hillside toward the top of the cave just out of the path of the sliding rock. Jim was ahead of her. He lifted Kim Sue out first and handed her to Kate and then he got Sheena.

"You're good girls," he said huskily. "Brave girls."

Squatting precariously on the steep slope, Kate tried to hug them both at once and fight the tears that seemed to keep blurring her vision.

The boulder, sliding ominously out of control, had stopped short of the bonfire, and there was a compulsion among them all to touch it as if they were patting a wild animal that was suddenly domesticated. Even Addie patted it and smiled a merry, crinkly smile at the group.

"How 'bout some of my fried pies, you all?" she asked.

Kate, examining scratches and scrapes on the girls' legs and a cut on Kim Sue's cheek, said, "I'm gon' get you all bathed and in bed." Then she stopped.

What bed? She certainly didn't intend to let them

spend the night in that silver cabin within range of crazy Addie.

"I'm gon' take Addie into protective custody, if it's any help," said the sheriff. "Lorena's neighbor is my matron and she has a secure place for women prisoners in her house."

"Good," said Addie. "I'll feed my bird and be ready. Lucy's house is just one block from Wal-Mart. I'll take my list."

"I'm gon' take Kate and these girls into protective custody, too," said Edie. "Mama and I have plenty of room and plenty of hot water and maybe some hot soup."

Kate smiled at her gratefully. She looked around at all the people who had come out in the cold rainy twilight to help rescue the two girls—Jim and Smokey, the firemen, the wrecker driver, the bulldozer operator, the sheriff, PawPaw, and the whole colorful procession of townspeople in trucks and cars on the road.

"I wish I could do something to say thank you to you all," she said. "If you go to Pearlie's, I'll treat you to a hot supper."

PawPaw lifted an eyebrow and Lorena said, "I bet a cold drink would suit better."

Kate gulped. "Yes! But where? Is there a pub or a bar or something in town?"

"How about a couple of six-packs at the fire station?" one of the firemen said. "We'll send the bill to you."

"I wish I could go with you," said Kate, "but ... " She looked at the girls, who were leaning against her sleepily, and it moved her that Kim Sue, although a big girl, was clinging tight to her skirt. "I'm a little tied down now," she said.

They did stop by the jail to see if there was any word from the search party looking for Return. There was none. But the photographer Shell had sent was there, and Kate's heart sank when she saw him tilted back in the sheriff's chair with the sheriff's phone tucked between his shoulder and his ear and his feet on the sheriff's desk. She liked photographers almost better than anybody she had to work with, having had decades of happy association with them. But this one, an import from some Ivy League school in the East, thought himself far too good for the job and the region, a totally arrogant and pompous fraud. His pictures were far from exceptional; his attitude was infuriating. He never said he came from New York but always from Westchester County, which, Kate assumed, was a far more elegant reach of the city. He didn't plan to stay long—only till his "old man" returned from business commitments around the world and fixed him up with network television.

Meanwhile, his L. L. Bean all-weather boots remained on the sheriff's desk and his hand-knit virgin wool cap remained on his silken blond head. He waved at Kate and the sheriff imperiously and brought his conversation to a leisurely end. Then he got to his feet.

"Glad you could make it, Kate," he said, as if she were the tardy arrival. "Couldn't find you at that Blue Hole the assignment mentioned, so I went out on my own. Shot some of the scenery.

"The mountains up here aren't bad, are they? I got a few shots of the legislators and cavers along that bleak briar patch they call Scratch Ankle. That about wind it up? Not much happening, is there? I'd like to shove off."

"Not much happening!" Kate wanted to hit him. "Just murder and lost people and blood and . . . and . . . " She grasped the corner of the desk to try to pull herself together and tell him about Representative Pickett's bloody trailer.

Finally she said in disgust, "Go back and shoot that trailer." And then, realizing there had been no introductions, she said, "Sheriff Atkins, this is Chris Mallory of our staff. Are the tapes still up at the scene or can Chris take a picture in the trailer?"

The sheriff, who had better manners than the elegant import from the East, shook hands and said, "The tapes are still up, Kate, but I could let him shoot from the door as long as he doesn't touch anything. I think the crew from the crime lab finished, but I don't want to risk disturbing anything."

"You heard that, Chris," Kate said severely. "You will photograph, not touch."

"Gotcha," said the boy with a smile so charming it was hard to believe it was on the face of an incompetent jerk. "Sheriff, how about being a good scout and taking me to the scene?" he asked patronizingly.

Kate grimaced in embarrassment, but the sheriff smiled.

"I'll ask my deputy, Mr. King, to accompany you," he said with unaccustomed formality.

"I think you'd better plan to stay tonight," Kate said. "If they find Representative Pickett or his body, the other newspapers and television will be jumping on the story. We should have a photographer here."

"Okay, so while I'm gone get me a room, will you?"

Kate's smile was warm. "I'll be glad to. There's a charming motel called 'Home in the Pines' down there on Scratch Ankle Road. I already have a room paid for there, a pretty silver one, but I have other plans. You may have it."

Edie was smiling, too, visualizing this foppish fellow in the unheated silver shack on this cold night trying to cope with the woodstove. "I'll get you a key," she said.

As they were leaving, Kate asked curiously, "Chris, how did you happen to get this assignment?"

"Small Sunday staff and everybody out but me. Besides, this is probably page one and they kind of like to have me on the good stuff."

"In a pig's eye," Kate muttered to herself. She collected the little girls, who were lumped together and dozing on the sheriff's sofa, and propelled them toward her car. Edie had pointed out the house she shared with her mother two blocks away. Its lighted windows looked warm and welcoming.

Kate did like photographers; she apologized to herself for her scornful attitude toward this one. Some of them were very brave, risking their lives at fires and shootouts and tornadoes and hurricanes and wrecks. They worked hard, not complaining about long hours and bad weather, and were usually fun, good company. Why did she have to have a gruesome one on this gruesome assignment?

Edie's house, an old-fashioned, vaguely Victorian white frame, was really her mother's and it almost made up for the rigors of the day. Mrs. Putnam, herself a retired teacher, received them with old-fashioned courtesy, offering her hand to Kate and to each of the girls—a grown-up attention they enjoyed in spite of being exhausted, hungry, and pinched with cold.

"I'm gon' show you your beds and the bathroom and give you a chance to freshen up," she said, using Kate's favorite genteelism for going to the bathroom. "Then I want you to come straight to the kitchen and have some of my soup." She leaned toward the girls and in a conspiratorial whisper said, "I made brownies this afternoon."

Kim Sue promptly burst into tears and clutched at Kate. In a second Sheena, although avowedly too big to cry, swallowed hard and tears came in her eyes.

"Oh, Mrs. Putnam," Kate began an awkward apology, but Edie interrupted. "I'll explain to Mother, Kate. The girls have gone through a thoroughly traumatic experience and it all began when that crazy Addie Armentrout told them she had some fried pies. They'll probably never want another goodie as long as they live."

"Yes, they will," said Kate, using her shirttail to wipe their faces and smiling at them. "That turned out bad, but they know they're safe now. They're just real tired. I can't wait to try some of Mrs. Putnam's soup."

The girls followed Kate into the bedroom, crowding close to her, but Kim Sue turned at the door and ventured a forgiving smile in Mrs. Putnam's direction.

The rooms in this house were big and the guest room assigned to Kate and the girls had wide matching spool beds, three-quarter in size, if not double. They were covered with crocheted counterpanes over flowered chintz dust ruffles, which matched draperies over white nylon curtains at the windows. There was a dressing table with a flouncy flowered skirt and a mirror encircled in dried corsages, spoils of Edie's teenage years, Kate thought.

Edie saw and interpreted Kate's look at the corsages and shook her head.

"My niece. I never got enough flowers to frame a compact mirror. Ugly duckling."

"Well, you're not that now," said Kate, steering the girls toward the connecting bathroom and a vast legged tub which somebody was filling with hot water foaming with bubble bath.

"That's how Turn felt," said Edie softly.

Kate busied herself pulling T-shirts over the girls' heads.

"I should have guessed," she said. "You were in love."

"The term, Kate, is lovers."

"Did anybody know?"

"In these small towns? Rising Fawn and Pudding Hill?"

"And Scratch Ankle and New Salem and Hog Jowl Road?" threw in Kate, grinning. "You mean privacy was nonexistent. Except from your mother, I suppose. She doesn't know."

"Unwritten code," said Edie. "Nobody tells anybody's mother. They find out sometimes—by osmosis, I reckon. Mother liked Turn and would have been proud to have

Cherokee grandchildren, but we hadn't come to that point yet. He had this obsession about his ancestors and that land and I'm not even sure he would want to marry anybody but some dusky Minnehaha."

"I can't believe that," Kate said. "I don't suppose I dare say he's so thoroughly American. That's considered chauvinistic now and of course everybody makes a point of the fact that his ancestors got here first. But I did have a couple of beers with him after the legislature one afternoon and I didn't feel any prejudice against . . . the rest of us."

They both smiled wryly at Kate's inability to simply say "white people." But Edie's freckled face was shadowed with unhappiness. She turned to her room across the wide hall and returned with nightdresses for Kate and the girls, the little ones her own, the bigger one her mother's.

When the girls were clean and dry and enveloped in the only-slightly-too-big gowns, they filed into the big bright kitchen where an enormous oil burner sent out heat and an iron Dutch oven on the stove sent out the fragrance of beef and vegetable soup. Places were set at a round oak table in the middle of the room.

"Sit down, sit down," urged Mrs. Putnam. "The corn bread is ready to come out of the oven. You girls want milk? Kate—may I call you Kate? I read your column!— you may have coffee, tea, buttermilk, or some of my muscadine wine with your dinner. It's nice and dry."

Sleet lashed against the big kitchen windows and Kate could hear a chill north wind slicing at the roof.

"Wine," she said promptly.

The soup was good, the kind only a meaty knuckle bone simmered for days and homegrown vegetables could make, and the brownies were well filled with pecans, which the girls couldn't pass up.

The girls went off to bed content and were sound asleep within moments. Kate, wrapped in one of Mrs. Putnam's robes over the borrowed nightgown, went to sit in the living room with the other two women, thinking there might be something on the news about Pickett and probably a mention that Representative Banks was missing, if that was still true. The sheriff had an idea that he had wandered away from the search party and was only temporarily lost. Listening to the wind and the crackle of the sleet, Kate hoped he had been found or had found shelter in one of the many caves.

"Could the cavers possibly be out there still looking in this weather?" she asked.

"If there's a chance of finding either of them dead or alive, they're out there," said Edie. "I saw Jim rescue a girl when the temperature was seven degrees. Rescue work is one of the important things about being a caver."

The recital of humdrum television news by a handsome young man with an unctuous chocolate-flavored delivery was suddenly interrupted for a bulletin. Two legislators were missing in the Scratch Ankle area tonight, one of them believed to be dead, since there were bloodstains and evidence of a struggle in his trailer home. The other disappeared while a member of the search party.

It went on from there.

"Chris better get his pictures to the office right away," said Kate, standing up. "I need to find him and tell him the competition has come to life."

"You can't get him on Addie's phone, you know," said Edie. "She's a sort of prisoner at Lucy's. Her office is locked up tight except for that window I broke. He wouldn't hear or answer the phone anyway, would he?"

"Probably not," said Kate. "I'll have to go find him. He can transmit from Chattanooga, I suppose."

"Let me go," said Edie. "You better stay with the girls. They'll be frightened if they wake up and you aren't here."

Kate paused.

"I know, but I don't want you prowling around out there in that weather looking for our photographer. It's my job. The girls know you and I think they'll feel safe with you and your mother. Besides, they're so tired I don't believe they'll wake up."

"Child, you can't go," Mrs. Putnam spoke up unexpectedly from her recliner close to the television set. "I put yours and the children's clothes in the washing machine."

"Well, thank you," said Kate, "but..."

The three of them gave way to helpless laughter.

"There must be something I can wear," Kate said, looking distractedly around the room.

"Don't look at our green velvet drapes, Scarlett," said Edie.

They laughed again and Mrs. Putnam got to her feet. "I have a hunting suit that belonged to my husband. I bet it will fit you."

And it did, loosely enough to be comfortable over the long underwear, which was Mrs. Putnam's.

"Now my jacket," said Kate.

"Oh, it's washable, too," said Mrs. Putnam. "I read the label. You know how muddy it was."

Kate wanted to shake her for a meddlesome old lady, but she looked at the distress on the soft pink face and she hugged her instead.

"I'll be fine without it. My car has a heater, and besides, this is a pretty warm outfit."

"Not warm enough," said Mrs. Putnam. "Wait a minute. I have something that will be plenty big."

She returned with a fur coat.

"Oh, no!" gasped Kate. "I can't take your nice coat."

"You certainly can," said Mrs. Putnam. "I don't wear it much anymore since Edie came home with one of those signs about killing helpless animals. Here."

She draped it over Kate's shoulders and Kate reluctantly shoved her arms into the satin-lined, lavender-smelling sleeves.

The sleet on the roof was making staccato Krupa-on-drums sounds as Kate reached the porch.

"Here's Papa's cap," said Edie, running out with a khaki hunting cap. "It has earflaps. Warmer than a head scarf and will turn the rain."

Gratefully Kate pushed her hair up under the cap, saluted, and ran for her car. In spite of the sleet beating

against the windshield, she had no trouble finding
Scratch Ankle Road and the sad little tourist court,
although there were no streetlights and certainly no
lighted sign to advertise its presence. But to her surprise,
when she drove in the yard one of the cabins had a light
in the window and smoke pluming out of its small chim-
ney. It was not the silver one she had rented but on farther down the line—the purple one, for goodness' sake!

Kate smiled to herself, thinking how hath the mighty
Westchester County boy fallen. She touched the horn
and opened the door, preparing to slide out into the
sleety night.

The cabin door opened and a man's voice—but not
Chris's—called out gruffly, "You sure took your time!"

"What?" said Kate, fighting a creepy feeling that the
cabins were haunted.

"Git on in here," said the voice, "and git off that coat."

"Not on your life!" yelled Kate. "Not on a night like
this!"

She slammed the car door, started the engine, and
skidded out of the driveway. A mile down the road she
slowed down and watched the rearview mirror. No following lights. There had been something familiar about that
voice and she felt that the meeting in the purple cabin
was to have been more than a lovers' tryst. On impulse
she turned into a rocky weed-grown clearing off the road
and doused her lights. She didn't know what kind of car
she was expecting, because Addie or some other owner
when it was the No Tell Inn had obligingly arranged hidden parking spaces back of the cabins to protect the cus-

tomers from the eyes of the curious, especially curious spouses. She had not seen a car.

If she had had time, she would have backed the car into the briar patch instead of nosing it in, so she would have been in position to follow speedily when the car appeared. But she never had been good at backing up and that rocky spot was less road than ledge, with a steep fall on either side. Better to wait as she was, damning her capricious heater for quitting so promptly when the engine was off, and drawing the collar of Mrs. Putnam's coat closer around her neck.

After twenty minutes no car had appeared and Kate started trying to remember the way the old road wound down the mountain. Was there an exit at the other end? She seemed to recall a narrow dirt road past a collection of little houses which had been occupied by miners up until the mines went out of business in the 1920s or '30s. They were sad little houses but probably no sadder now than in the days when the mines operated and living was hard and dirty.

The man in the purple cabin had either gone back to bed or taken the road to the shoddy little mining shacks or beyond. Kate started the car, wondering why she had waited anyhow. The tailing technique might be good for catching murderers, but she suspected all she would be catching would be some married man who picked the worst night of the year for his philandering.

Meanwhile, where was Chris, that photographer?

She had not checked the silver cabin, but it was obviously untenanted—closed up, unlighted, unheated.

She drove to the sheriff's office. It was brightly lighted. She could see through the window a number of people standing around. In a town which numbered among its charms the fact that motorists could always find a parking space, she couldn't find one near the jail. She drove around the block and came up on a side street, relieved to make out—in spite of the darkness and the sleet, which seemed to be turning to snow—a white car with her newspaper's logo on the door.

Praise be, she thought, *home and mother! Somebody will be here—Chris, if all else fails—but possibly another reporter and a good photographer.* She reached the corner of the building and was about to turn toward the main street when something grazed the collar of Mrs. Putnam's coat—something hard, moving fast and so hot it scorched the fur.

It struck the building beyond her and Kate started running. She had been shot at!

As she mounted the steps, she heard a car roar off.

The door to the sheriff's office was standing open and she barely made it in, collapsing on the old sofa in speechless shock.

Sheriff Atkins was standing back of his desk with a coffee cup in his hand. He took one look at Kate and strode over to her.

"You're white as a sheet—" he began.

Kate nodded. "Been shot at. Somebody just shot at me," she quavered.

"Where? How long ago?"

"A minute ago. Right outside."

"Come on," the sheriff said to the others, grabbing his jacket and running for the door.

"Too late," said Kate. "He's gone. The car raced off before I even got to the steps outside. You'd never catch it."

The sheriff turned back. "Anybody hear whose car that was?"

"I did," said Lorena morosely, leaning into her covered typewriter. "But I don't know whose car it was. Not for sure."

CHAPTER THREE

KATE STARTED OUT the door with the sheriff and his deputy, followed by a gallery of cavers and Chris, the photographer. Too late to find the gunman, they were hoping to find the bullet and perchance where it hit the courthouse wall. Kate wanted to see, too, but the smell of scorched hair around her neck stopped her. She had indeed been shot at, crazy as it seemed. She had been shot at and the bullet had come close!

She took off Mrs. Putnam's coat and draped it over the sheriff's desk. Lorena was enabled by a sudden surge of energy to get to her feet and come and look over Kate's shoulder.

"You wasn't kidding," she muttered. "Come close."

"And whoever shot at me," Kate said, managing a grin, "wasn't kidding, either. But why? Why?"

"Maybe you hurt somebody's feelings," Lorena suggested idly, returning to her chair back of the typewriter."

Kate stared at her. "Is that the Rising Fawn way, to shoot anybody who hurts your feelings?"

Lorena shrugged and resumed her seat.

The sheriff came in with an envelope in his hand. "Thirty-eight pistol," he said. "We got the bullet."

"The kind everybody in Dade County has," said one of the cavers.

"I think it had a silencer," said Kate. "At least I didn't hear it."

"Not many folks have silencers," the same caver said.

The sheriff saw Mrs. Putnam's coat laid out damply on his desk. "I'm gon' have to ask you to leave your coat with us," he said. "I know it's a cold night, but this is evidence."

Kate nodded. "I know, but it isn't my coat. I borrowed it from Edie's mother. I was going—" Suddenly she remembered where she had been going. "To find you, Chris," she said to the photographer, who was hovering in the doorway, his camera trained on the coat.

"Put it back on, Kate," he said. "Let me get a picture."

Kate started to protest. She hated pictures of herself. But this was news, she knew, and it would be unfair for her to ask other people in the news to do what she wouldn't do herself.

"Okay, Sheriff?" asked Chris with a new turn toward manners.

"Go ahead, but be careful of the collar." He held the coat out to Kate to slip her arms in, and carefully spread the collar so the photographer could get the brown runnel of scorched fur across the middle.

"I was looking for you, Chris, to tell you that this story is already on television and up for grabs and to be sure you knew so you could rush your pictures back to the office. Did you get anything at the trailer?"

The young photographer looked smug. "Everything. Pretty gory, huh?"

"Next question. Did you bring a portable so you can transmit from here, or do you have to go to Chattanooga?"

"I guess it's Chattanooga. AP bureau? And Kate, is it okay if I get a room there somewhere? I saw that silver junk you paid for... honestly, kid!"

"You did?" said Kate eagerly. "What time were you there? Did you see anybody else there?"

"Nope. The place was a graveyard."

Kate turned to the sheriff. "I went there looking for Chris and a man came out of the purple cabin and snarled at me, ordering me to take off my coat and come in. I left."

The sheriff looked unimpressed. "It's been that kind of place where ladies and gentlemen meet."

Turning to the cavers, he said, "Boys, why don't you call it a day? It's too wet and too dark to keep searching tonight. Anybody lost on the mountain has likely found a cave by now."

Kate thought of the cave Kim Sue and Sheena had "found" and stirred restively. "I'd better go," she said, taking off the coat and handing it to the sheriff.

"Lorena," said the sheriff, "get a blanket from the jail and let Kate wrap up in it for the trip to Mrs. Putnam's."

Lorena was slow to get up and Kate said her car was close and she would be warm enough for the short trip. It was enough for Lorena, who had started to rise and then settled back, looking, Kate thought, like some primitive household god, who sat motionless, unwinking in the corner. And the sheriff had said she "ran" the office!

Chris walked to the staff car as Kate headed toward her car. She prided herself on never asking for special care or consideration from her male colleagues, but she turned down the dark street wishing that some able-bodied man was along to be sure no .38-toting strangers were waiting for her. She wished fleetingly for the screwdriver and pliers she habitually carried in her pocket when she was investigating a crime. They had on occasion fooled some street slicker into thinking she packed a gun. But how did she know to prepare for crime here? And how did she know she was the intended victim of a crime?

The backseat of her car was dark but blessedly unoccupied and she hurried to start the engine and pull out into the lighted street. There was space for her car in the driveway back of Mrs. Putnam's house, but she stopped at the curb thinking it looked very dark back there. While she hesitated, a floodlight went on in the backyard and she gratefully pulled in off the street and parked next to Edie's red Blazer and her mother's sedate blue Oldsmobile. Both Edie and her mother met her at the kitchen door, holding it open so the warm, food-fragrant air rushed out to meet her.

Kate stumbled tiredly up the back steps and to the welcoming arms of the two women.

"We worried, honey," said Mrs. Putnam. "You were gone a long time for a trip to Addie's place."

"Oh, it was more complicated than that," said Kate, "and how nice of you to worry about me and not about your coat. You see I'm not wearing it."

"You had to hide it in a cave to keep animal lovers from spraying it with yellow paint, didn't you?" joked Edie.

"It's all right," said Mrs. Putnam. "Whatever happened, I don't care. Just so long as you are safe. Those precious girls haven't even turned over once since they went to bed. Come on and let me fix you a snack or something."

"Let me fix you a drink," said Edie, helping to unzip the khaki hunting suit and lifting the rain- and sleet-soggy hunting cap from Kate's head. "I don't mean Mother's muscadine wine, either. Something stronger. What do you normally drink in fiendish weather?"

"Oh, a cup of tea will be fine," said Kate, stepping out of her wet shoes.

"Good girl," said Mrs. Putnam, collecting the wet clothes. "We'll put a little rum and honey in it."

In the living room the television still hadn't revealed the full extent of the dire happenings at Scratch Ankle. Edie said they had mentioned the missing legislators—but perfunctorily—and gone ahead with an old movie starring Alice Faye, Don Ameche, and Tyrone Power.

"Good, too," said Mrs. Putnam, spreading an afghan over Kate's shoulders as Edie handed her a steaming mug which telegraphed its contents with the fine smell of honey and rum.

Kate told them of the man at the motel and the shooting just outside the country courthouse, attempting to apologize for the damage to Mrs. Putnam's coat and the fact that it might be months before she saw it again.

"Don't you give it a thought, child," the older woman said. "I feel guilty every time I put that thing on and now that it's been shot at I can wear it with pride."

Kate tried to insist that when the sheriff released it she would take it to a furrier and have the collar replaced.

"You'll do nothing of the kind," said Mrs. Putnam, standing up. "Now I'm going to bed and you and Edie can talk."

Kate was so tired she didn't think she was up to more talk, but one look at the pain on Edie's freckled face was sufficient to keep her up and trying.

"Have you heard anything more from the search?" she asked.

Edie shook her head. "Jim and Smokey are still out there. They've looked in all the big well-known caves. Jim called from some farmer's house up on Sand Mountain. They alerted everybody up there. Even checked out some abandoned buildings, including a church. But they were going back into the wilds where they may have overlooked some of the smaller caves and some of the places like Shelter Rock where hunters sometimes get in out of the weather and build campfires. I don't think there's any hope of finding Turn, do you, Kate?"

Kate hadn't thought there was any hope of finding

Turn alive since she saw his trailer and especially that scuffed-up section of trail where the leaves bore evidence of a bloody struggle. She couldn't say that to Edie. Instead she asked who would want the young legislator dead.

"I can't think of anybody," Edie said. "I've racked my brain all day. He was popular enough to win the race for the legislature—almost overwhelmingly. He was friends with all the cavers, and people in town thought a lot of him. He supported all our good causes like the historical society and the library. He didn't go to church—but have you ever heard of killing somebody because they didn't go to church?"

"Maybe some places in the world, but not in the Georgia mountains," Kate said.

"I've even thought of other women," Edie said softly. "It was presumptuous of me to assume I was the only one, I guess. I thought maybe in Atlanta or somewhere else there might be a girl. But I can't believe that, really. We were so close . . . so much in love!" Her voice broke and she ducked her head and pushed at her eyes with the backs of her hands.

"Oh, it's absurd to even think he had a relationship with a woman that would come to this horrible pass," said Kate with more conviction than she felt.

Edie smiled tremulously. "You know that's what I want to believe. I don't know how I can go on without him. He was interested in so many things and taught me so much. We hiked a lot and camped out and he knew all kinds of woodlore I never dreamed of in all the years I've lived in

97

the mountains. Besides that . . . " She paused and bit her lip and her eyes filled with tears, "he was so gentle and sweet."

Kate wanted to cry for her, this kind little schoolteacher who had met a good man and fallen in love and lost it all so fast. Kate had known Benjy Mulcay most of her life, since their fathers were on the Atlanta police force together and they went as children to department picnics in Grant Park. They had had time to fight and squabble and hate each other and grow up and fall in love and embark on an adventurous twenty-year marriage. This girl—this nice brave generous girl—had had, what, two years? Kate felt guilty to have had so much.

Edie sat next to her on the sofa and Kate put an arm around her. "I'm sorry, honey," was all she could think to say.

"I keep thinking," said Edie, "that if he's alive, he's in terrible pain somewhere out there on the mountain. I just hope that you will help us find whoever did this awful thing. I know you have had experience in catching killers."

"Nothing like this, not ever," said Kate. "You've got better people—experts in Jim and Smokey. But if there's anything I can do . . . "

"I know," said Edie. "And I love you for it." She blew her nose and stood up. "You go to bed. It's been a long day and you must be dead on your feet."

Kate was tired, so shaky from weariness she staggered a bit as she walked toward the guest room. At the door she turned. Edie was locking the front door.

"We never do this," she said. "As long as I can remember, I've thought that key was for decoration. But tonight ..."

"Lock it," said Kate. "How about the back door?"

"I'll get it, too."

Kate stood in the hall and watched as Edie turned keys and extinguished lights.

"How about Representative Banks? Any word on him?"

Edie shook her head. She paused in the dim light of the hall. "I wonder," she said, "if he and Turn were together on anything down at the capitol? Could it be the same people were after both of them?"

Kate looked at her reflectively. It was something she hadn't thought of. Tomorrow ... if she could only sleep a bit she'd think about it.

"Go on," said Edie. "The covers are turned back. There's a comforter at the foot if you need it. Sleep as late as you like. Mother and I go to church, but you'll find breakfast makings in the kitchen."

Kate meant to think about the question Edie had raised, but she only had time to appreciate the silky feel of Mrs. Putnam's percale sheets and the softness of real down pillows before she slept.

Kate awakened to the sound of church bells. The girls had retrieved from the car their zipper bag, which Kate had forgotten about, and were dressed in their Sunday best—flowered nylon, over which they wore their red and blue zipper jackets and beneath which they wore the mud-stained running shoes of the day before.

The effect was ludicrous, but Mrs. Putnam winked at Kate and said they looked fine and were going to church with her.

"The Pepper family belongs to our church and they're going to be singing today. I knew the girls would want to hear them. How about you? Would you like to go?"

"Mother, let her rest," put in Edie, also dressed for church. "I bet Kate never heard of the Pepper family and would rather have a leisurely cup of coffee, no matter how pretty they sing."

Kate, wrapped in Mrs. Putnam's robe, grinned grate-fully. "I would, Edie, I really would like to go with you all, but it would be wonderful to take my time over a cup of coffee. If you'll excuse me, Mrs. Putnam?"

"Of course, honey," said Mrs. Putnam over a mouthful of pins she was using to pull Kim Sue's hair into a sem-blance of Sunday smoothness. "Coffee's on the stove, biscuits in the oven, and your clean clothes are on that table in the bathroom. Take your time and we'll see you in about an hour."

Kate thought of a leisurely soak in the big tub but gave coffee priority. She took her cup to the living room and looked first for the Atlanta newspaper. The Putnams sub-scribed to the *Chattanooga Times*. It was open to the front page and there was a five-paragraph story about the two missing legislators. No mention of blood and possi-ble murder. Apparently lost campers and hikers were rou-tine weekend happenings on Lookout Mountain and the supposition was that they would turn up sooner or later, safe and happy to have had a taste of exceptional scenery.

Kate was on her second cup of coffee when she heard a thud on the front porch and peered out the hall window to see the Atlanta paper.

Bless the Putnams, she thought, they have taste. No polyester sheets on their beds, no day without their capital city newspaper. She pulled the paper out of its plastic case and opened it to find her story and Chris's pictures on page one.

The rain and sleet had let up. The sun was shining outside and Kate felt the inner lightness and brightness which came from having scooped another newspaper with a page one story.

But the feeling speedily passed. It was a superficial attitude from her competitive youth. Now she faced a far more serious—remembering Edie—tragic situation. She took her cup to the kitchen and washed and dried it and hurried to the bathroom, not for the leisurely soak she had wanted, but for a quick wash, tooth brushing, and hair combing. Dressed in the slacks and shirt Mrs. Putnam had washed for her, she sought the kitchen telephone. There was another one in the hall, but she had developed an affection for the big warm kitchen with its cushioned ladder-back chairs and big rocker. It now smelled enticingly of Sunday roast and under a clean towel on the counter there was an apple pie Mrs. Putnam must have made before dawn.

She dialed the sheriff's office.

"You brought them down on us, Kate," the sheriff said. "Two television crews and Lord knows how many reporters are here. I sent a batch of them over to Pearlie's for breakfast. I expect there'll be more as the day goes along."

"Did our phtographer, Chris, make it back or call in?" Kate asked.

"He was asleep on my sofa when I left home at five o'clock. Said there wasn't a thing in Chattanooga. We got that boy broke in. He would have been glad to spend the night in a jail cell if I hadn't taken him home with me."

Kate laughed. "A little murder makes troupers out of the worst of us."

"Speaking of which"—the sheriff's tone turned serious—"you're some trouper yourself. We haven't got the first line on whoever that was shot at you. We got to figure he was either a poor shot or was just trying to scare you."

"Well, it was dark back there in your alley," Kate said thoughtfully. "I'm not even sure where it came from. There were a lot of cars parked back there."

"My guess is he thought you were somebody else."

Kate heard the voices of arriving reporters and television crews. She didn't want to share what she was thinking with anybody else. She got up, put on her jacket, and headed for her car in the backyard. The churchgoers were just arriving in Mrs. Putnam's blue Oldsmobile.

The girls were singing melodiously, not one of the Pepper family's stellar hymns but the sweet ballad "Fair and Tender Ladies." The place was exercising charm on them in spite of the dire happenings.

Edie and Mrs. Putnam shepherded them toward the back steps. Kate pulled Edie aside.

"Where does Lorena live?"

"Just down the street," said Edie. "Why?"

"Something I need to ask her," Kate said.

"Go ahead," said Mrs. Putnam. "The girls are going to change their clothes and help me put out seed for my birds. That rain last night washed away every grain I had on the feeders and the birds are hungry. Then we gon' put dinner on the table and we want you to be back for that, hear?"

"Yes, ma'am" Kate said meekly. "You girls all right? Did you enjoy church?"

"Yes, *ma'am!*" they said together. "Mommer ain't gon' believe we got to see the Peppers in person. We even got autographs!" They held up church programs to show her.

"Well, I'm gon' run down the street and see Miss Lorena. You know, from the sheriff's office? You'll be okay here with Mrs. Putnam till I get back?"

Sheena looked accepting but uncertain. They had had enough of being left behind after their experience with Addie Armentrout. Still, they recognized, as Kate herself did, how seductive comfort and food were and the charms of putting sunflower seeds out for all the birds which gathered around the colorful assemblage of bird-houses and bird feeders encircling Mrs. Putnam's back-yard.

"We'll wait for you," Sheena finally said. "Just so you don't be too long."

Amused at having obtained permission, Kate walked up the street toward the brick ranch house Edie had pointed out as Lorena's. It had aluminum awnings in morose dirt-smudged stripes of maroon sheltering the doorway and front windows. Last night's rainwater and melted sleet dripped sibilantly from the scallops. A little dog barked hysterically as Kate mounted the steps. She rang the bell and after an interminable wait the door opened and Lorena stood there naked, clutching a purple satin gown to her chest in a pitiful attempt at cover. Her blue-black hair, pulled from its glued cone, sprangled out in all directions. Her sagging breasts, her face, and her arms were a mass of lacerations rapidly turning the same blue-black color of her hair. A little white dog circled her bare feet and leaped at her frantically before racing out the open door.

"Lorena!" cried Kate. "What on earth happened to you?"

The battered woman swayed and grabbed at the door for support.

"It was me, not you, he was after," she whispered. "I told him I wouldn't tell."

"Who?" demanded Kate. "Tell what?"

But Lorena swayed again and toppled to the floor.

Oh, let it be a faint, Kate prayed silently, kneeling to feel her pulse. She couldn't find it. She never could seem to find her own pulse, much less anybody else's. She looked around distractedly for a telephone. There was one beside a badly tumbled bed in the front room. She tried to reach it and punch in 911 without touching anything. Obviously somebody had pulled Lorena out of her bed and beaten her viciously. Maybe fatally. The sheriff answered the emergency number himself, now that he didn't have Lorena there to do it for him.

"I'll be right there," he said. "Do we need an ambulance?"

"I don't know," Kate faltered. "I'm afraid so. A doctor anyway."

The fire department's rescue van arrived almost as fast as the sheriff did and had lifted Lorena to a stretcher and were taking her out the door in a matter of minutes. The sheriff followed along, holding Lorena's hand and chafing it anxiously.

"What is it, Lo? What happened? Who hurt you?"

The snarl of blue-black hair turned restlessly. The eyes back of the swollen blue-black pouches did not open.

Kate stood in the doorway looking after them. If she had only thought, she would have put a robe or something on Lorena. It was awful sending the bruised flesh off uncovered for all to see when they lifted the ambulance sheet and blanket.

The sheriff turned and came back up the walk. "What happened?"

"I don't know," said Kate. "I came to ask her. She said the shot aimed at me was intended for her. And then she fainted."

The young sheriff sighed deeply. "It doesn't let up, does it? Well, I'm gon' have to lock the door and call the experts again. There's bound to be something. What did he hit her with? He must have touched something. Fingerprints. Tracks. We better get out of here."

Kate stood in the bedroom door looking at the mess a beating made: tangled sheets, blanket on the floor, a lamp shaped like a rooster dangling from a cord over the bed, a SEE ROCK CITY shag rug pushed to one side.

"Sheriff," she asked, "who was Lorena seeing? Who gave her that fur coat?"

The young man turned from an inspection of the kitchen. "You know, I don't know. We kidded her about it, but she never would say. When she was younger Lorena wasn't bad-looking and she got around quite a bit. Some thought she was . . . " he fumbled for a word and came out with an old-fashioned one, "fast. She had to help a bunch of relatives. Used to live out Scratch Ankle Road and I thought what she did on her own time was none of my business."

"Let me ask a favor," said Kate. "Let me look at her fur coat."

The sheriff looked puzzled and reluctant, but after a pause he said, "I reckon it's all right. See if it's in her closet. And don't touch it any more than you can help."

Kate didn't know if the plastic cleaner's bag would hold fingerprints, so she slipped her hand up under it without touching the outside. The label was what she wanted to see and after a moment she was able to pull it to the edge of the plastic.

The sheriff, watching, said suddenly, "I see what you're looking for. You had on that fur coat and whoever shot that pistol thought you were Lorena in hers. What does the label tell you?"

"I hope the name of the store where he bought the coat," Kate said. "Do you know Isaacson, Furriers?"

The sheriff shook his head. "But we can sure find out."

They left together, the sheriff to go to the hospital and

check on Lorena and once again activate the scene-of-the-crime crew from Atlanta. Kate turned back to Mrs. Putnam's to check on Kim Sue and Sheena. Edie had packed a lunch to take to the searching party at Blue Hole and the girls, back in their jeans and T-shirts, were eager to get to the mountain and resume their search for Smokey the Bear. Mrs. Putnam had put a plate of Sunday dinner in the oven for Kate and gone to take a nap.

Kate sat at the kitchen table, but she had no appetite for the excellent roast and vegetables. She kept thinking about poor gaudy Lorena, who either cared too much about some man or was too afraid of him to name him and solve the whole bitter mess. Kate only belatedly remembered the little white dog and wondered if she should go find him.

When she told Edie about Lorena and the dog, Edie said, "Aw, we'll look later. Lorena is crazy about that pooch, but she lets her-him run outside a lot."

"You know, you said in a small town everybody knows everything about each other," Kate said. "Who was Lorena seeing? Who gave her that fur coat?"

Edie, busy at the sink filling a big Thermos jug with hot coffee, shook her head. "She used to be a rounder, going with anybody who would give her the time of day. But . . . well, you saw how she looks. Older and no longer pretty and I guess the whole town was amazed when she stepped out in that fur coat. But I don't think anybody knows where it came from. Lorena wasn't saying and the man, if he was from around here, sure kept a low profile."

"I guess we can find out tomorrow," Kate said. "I

looked at the label and the coat came from Isaacson's, Would that be Chattanooga or Memphis or Atlanta?"

"It was Chattanooga," said Edie, "but they sold the store last summer. I don't know who the buyer was."

"Makes it harder," said Kate. "But not impossible. When the stores open tomorrow, we'll start trying."

Edie was gathering her gear for the trip back to the mountain and the girls couldn't tear themselves away from watching and inspecting it.

"You gon' plumb jump off the mountain, Miss Edie?" asked Sheena.

"Only after I have myself safe with these things," said Edie, smiling at them. "You see, you have this nice strong rope and you tie it to a tree—or two good stout trees if you can find them close. That's what we call 'anchoring it.' And then I have this seat sling made out of webbing and this rack and carabiner made out of steel. I'll weave the rope through these bars, over and under." She demonstrated. "That will let me down gradually."

The girls were losing interest.

"That rope don't look like nothing but a piece of clothesline to me," observed Sheena. "Mommer's got one runs between the corncrib and the chinaberry tree. I could git that and jump, couldn't I?"

"You certainly could not!" said Edie emphatically. "You could hurt yourself—break bones, even kill yourself. You wait, and when you are a little older you and Kim Sue can come up here and we'll teach you how to rappel. This is very special rope, made in only two counties in Georgia and used by fire departments and police departments and the Army and Navy and us. We'll get you some when you get bigger."

"Shit," said Kim Sue, and then recovered quickly. "I mean—"

"I know what you mean," Edie said. "And don't you let my mama hear you say that word. She'd wash your mouth out with soap."

"Yes'm," said Kim Sue. "But don't you git tard of having everything you want to do put off till you git old?"

Edie put down a seat sling she was preparing to pack in a nylon carryall and put an arm around the little girl.

"No, honey, when you are young you get to do things you can't do when you get old. The best thing is to enjoy everything as you go along."

Kim Sue sniffed and Kate turned away to keep from smiling. Kate's little neighbors were far more cynical and worldly than Edie. They most certainly had never heard of the scholar who said "Carpe diem" or "Seize the day," but they were natural believers in the rest of the line: "Put no trust in the morrow." They were born doubting.

With the picnic and rappelling gear loaded in the Blazer, they were ready to go until Mrs. Putnam hurried out on the porch in her housecoat. She motioned urgently for Edie and held her a moment in whispered conversation.

Edie laughed, bobbed her head, and rejoined Kate and the girls in her car.

"Something funny?" Kate asked.

Edie nodded. "Mama's funny. For an educated woman she's full of superstition and hocus-pocus. She'd die if she knew I told you, but she wanted me to go see Dr. Poultice."

"Poultice?" Kate repeated the name. "Polish, maybe?"

Edie shook her head. "Gosh, no! He was Georgia planter aristocracy originally, but he's been in these mountains eighty years or more. I forget what his real name is. Everybody calls him Dr. Poultice because he's an herb doctor and treats everything with poultices. He's also a sort of jackleg mystic. Finds lost dogs and cows and advises people about the phases of the moon. Mama thinks—"

"He might find Turn?" Kate interjected. "Let's go see him!"

Edie smiled and made a sharp left turn in the street. "Okay. If you want to. The cavers are probably already on the job, so I reckon we have time. Besides, he lives on the way."

"Here in town?"

"Certainly not! If you were into herbs and poultices would you live in this urban center?"

Kate looked at the little houses lining the main street, Pearlie's Café, the one grocery store, the neat little post office, the faded beauty of the Victorian courthouse with its small square of grass and borders of indefatigable pansies.

"T'wouldn't be fitting," she admitted.

"I hate to tell you where he lives," said Edie. "He didn't name it that, but he didn't try to change it. The name stuck. Sweet Love settlement. Out from, really. His house is not in metropolitan Sweet Love but beyond on a ridge."

"Sweet Love," marveled Kate, giggling. "I bet I know the origin. Beautiful Indian maiden, brave from another tribe. Sweet forbidden love."

Edie made a face. "You got us wrong. We may not be Yellowstone National Park, but we're not banal. There's not a Lover's Leap in the entire county."

At that moment a siren bleated behind them and Edie looked in her rearview mirror to see the sheriff's car. She pulled over to the curb.

The lanky young sheriff, his face troubled, walked toward them.

Edie rolled down her window. "You want us to get out with our hands up, Jeff?"

He smiled briefly, but the creases of care and unaccustomed responsibility remained on his sun-browned brow.

"Thought you'd want to know," he said. "Lorena's pretty bad. Damage to her kidneys and spleen. She's in intensive care. Can't see anybody."

Kate had a sudden thought. "Sheriff, have you got somebody who can stand guard at the hospital? You know nurses would probably let anybody who claimed to be kin get to her."

The sheriff looked thoughtful. "See what you mean," he said. "As you know, I only got one deputy and he's up yonder." He nodded toward the blue mountains which cupped the valley. "I reckon I could deputize somebody else."

"I would," said Kate. "Somebody big and strong who won't listen to any lies."

The sheriff gave a little salute and turned to his car. Edie turned into a narrow road that climbed toward the mountains.

"Tell me about this Dr. Poultice," said Kate.

"Doctor?" squeaked Kim Sue from the backseat. "We ain't going to no doctor, are we?"

"Not your kind of doctor," said Edie soothingly. "In fact, you don't need to see him at all. You all can wait in the car."

"We'll see," said Sheena, not wanting to lose any options.

Kate wanted to sort out the details of the crimes, which seemed to have multiplied with terrifying rapidity, but the beauty of the countryside distracted her. The road climbed steeply with a confusion of sharp curves. Sheer walls of sandstone rose on one side, and between the trees there was a panoramic view of the valley and, beyond it, another blue mountain. On any other day she would have wanted to park and get out and look, but today the press of the pains and the loss of the good people in this beautiful spot weighed on her. They had called it the "lost county" once, and now it seemed to be lost in troubles too big to handle. The boy sheriff, serving his first term and untrained for the complexities facing him, particularly moved her. And she had developed a real affection for Edie and her mother. Even Lorena, garish and bitter, living in her overstuffed, pretentious bungalow which reflected the neglect she felt applied to herself, had been kind enough to be concerned when the girls were locked in the cave. She had found Addie Armentrout and brought her to the scene with . . .

"Edie," Kate asked suddenly, "that man who came with Lorena to the Armentrout cabins—was that one of her lovers?"

"PawPaw?" said Edie. "Probably. He's the richest man in town and doesn't have to make do with the local product, but he's not choosy. He's even made passes at me."

"Well, that shows taste," said Kate, grinning. "Hasn't he a family? Where did he come from?"

"I don't know where he came from. It was a while back when I was at the university. He must have been married because he refers to somebody as 'the late Mrs.' Doesn't that sound like a wife? I don't believe he has had any visitors like sons and daughters, but he's right friendly with all the local people. Even made a start on caving, but he's not very good at it. Too fat, I think."

"What's his business?" Kate asked.

"Oh, everything," said Edie. "Lumber, textiles, the bank, even an automobile agency in the next county. He's into everything. Bought a big house on Lookout Mountain just outside Chattanooga but seems to spend all his time in Rising Fawn."

The road took a sudden turn and they were on top of the mountain.

"Oh, Edie, can we look?" cried Kate.

"Oooh, yes, ma'am!" said a voice from the backseat.

Edie obligingly pulled over to the side of the road. Kate and the children piled out and stood on the edge of

113

the slope where trees had been thinned to give a clear view of the valley with its little towns, the toy-sized railroad train puffing along, and the vast blue mountain beyond.

"Ain't it somepin?" murmured Sheena. "Ain't it really somepin?"

Edie smiled at her. "We like it a lot. But prepare yourself to see something totally different. The community of Sweet Love, Georgia!"

Half a mile down the road, almost hidden by trees and titanic boulders, there was a niche in the mountainside like an enormous room. Gray granite walls, silvered by spray from a waterfall, enclosed it on three sides. Small pointed cedars like Christmas trees grew at the base of the walls and here and there out of the rock itself.

"Sweet Love Quarry," said Edie. "Sandstone was quarried out years ago and some of the limestone. You see the white rock, girls? That's limestone and that's the reason for all the pretty cedar trees. They love limestone."

She had pulled to a stop in the road and Kate and the girls gazed upward in awe for several minutes before they saw what Edie called Sweet Love Village. Scattered over the enclosure, where they were probably sheltered from everything but the south wind, was an assortment of trailers and shacks in the most appalling state of dilapidation Kate had seen outside a city dump. Junked cars and tractors were piled high with kitchen garbage and old rags. The waterfall was crisscrossed with lines on which jeans and shirts and diapers flapped.

"Look, girls," said Edie, laughing. "That's some lady's

washing machine. Just hang your clothes under the falling water and let nature do the rest!"

Kate got over her astonishment in time to ask, "Does Dr. Poultice live in this place?"

"Oh, no," said Edie. "He's close—around the bend. But Sweet Lovers are his friends and he discourages any effort by environmentalists to disturb them. They live as they can, he says, and they aren't hurting anybody."

Around the bend on a shelf overlooking the valley was a small stone house surrounded by fruit trees and tidy cultivated beds of wild plants. It was neat and lovingly kept. Edie pulled into the gravel driveway beside a battered rust-raddled 1950 pickup truck.

"This is it," she said. "The domicile and the office of Dr. Poultice!"

As if the mention of his name had summoned him, a small white-bearded man in old Army fatigues stepped out the door. He was scrupulously clean but so old both he and his clothes looked as if they might have been faded in the wash.

"Ladies?" he said politely.

Edie got out of the car and introduced them all, including Sheena and Kim Sue.

"What can I do for you?" the old man asked. "Warts? Stomach upset? Lost property?"

"Lost people," Edie said. "And maybe murder. My mother, Edith Putnam, thinks you might solve it all."

"I know Mrs. Putnam very pleasantly," Dr. Poultice said. "She graciously invited me to speak to her students when she taught at the high school. Won't you come in?"

They started toward the back door, but he stopped them. "No. Come. You are front-door visitors and I want to show you my most precious possession."

He stopped at the corner of the stone house and pointed to the view. Tall pines and spruce framed the vista of mountain and valley. Nothing seemed to keep his little house from tumbling over the precipice except two great boulders thrusting out from the earth at either end of what appeared to be his dooryard. Beside one of these he had contrived a bench with a slab of slate, where Kate envisioned him watching the sunrise and sunset.

The old man looked at it with undiminished pride and affection.

"'Ah, the indescribable innocence and beneficence of nature!'" he murmured. "Do you know Thoreau? How I wish he had had the advantage of living in a spot like this! 'Of sun and wind and rain, of summer and winter,'" he went on, "'such health, such cheer, they afford forever!'"

"Thoreau again?" asked Kate.

"Still," the old man said. "It's part of the same passage. You know Henry David, too?"

"Not well," said Kate. "But I live in the country and I do enjoy him."

The faded blue eyes back of steel-rimmed glasses regarded her with approval.

"Well, do come in, please."

The smells of the little house were palpable—a grassy, weedy compound of herb and leaf scents, and something else Kate hadn't smelled in years, a coal fire burning on

the hearth. Bunches of dried plants Kate couldn't iden-
tify hung from the rough boards overhead. It was one
room, with bookshelves from floor to ceiling. Even at the
end where there was a sink and a row of apothecary jars
filled with colored liquid, there were more shelves of
books.

"It's so nice and warm," Kate said. "I haven't seen a
coal fire in a long, long time."

The old man pointed to a bucket full of coal at the
edge of the hearth. "See, I pick up coal more easily than
wood, which has to be sawed. These mountains are full
of coal, the leavings of miners who brutalized our land
and were themselves brutalized. Ten or twelve hours a
day in the bowels of the earth and they coughed and
spat their lungs away. Even the deer and foxes and quail
vanished. There was no redbud on the hills. Until . . .
until the owners thought the supply of coal had dimin-
ished and they moved away, leaving our people hungry
and broken. Then . . . " he paused and smiled, "the bats
returned."

It was an old theme with him, Kate realized, but looking at Edie's face, she knew they hadn't time for it. To
change the subject, she inspected his room again admir-
ingly but covertly for a door to a bedroom and possibly a
bathroom. The old man's eyes were on her.

"This is all there is," he said. "I have a bedroll in front
of the fireplace for my sleeping chamber and an outhouse
in the backyard for other purposes. I bathe under a waterfall nature provides over yonder." He pointed to a small
stream trickling off the mountain.

"Gollee, really?" gasped Sheena. "I wish we had a waterfall!"

"But ain't it cold?" demanded Kim Sue.

"Some days it is," said Dr. Poultice. "Then I postpone my ablutions."

The little girls weren't sure what he postponed, but if it happened to be baths, they were on his side.

"Please be seated," directed the old man. "I will bring refreshments. And we will talk."

Since his water supply was outside, Kate felt sure the glasses wouldn't be sparklingly clean, but it was not glasses he brought but a tray of small stoneware cups in a deep blue-gray. Lifting one, Kate remarked on their beauty.

"One of the lovely things our mountains produce," said the old man, gratified. "There is a pottery down in the valley run by a young woman who gave me these cups in exchange for some wild ferns. The juice of the male fern, you know, is efficacious against burns."

"No, I didn't know," said Kate. "I'm glad to learn it."

"I think I did know," said Edie. "I think my mother uses that remedy. Did you teach her?"

"Perhaps," said the old man, passing around his cups. "This is sassafras, sweetened with sourwood honey. I have some hives up the hill there."

His chairs were old mule-ear straight chairs with seats of woven white-oak splits. He made sure his visitors had one each and then he took one for himself.

"You are interested in botanic medicine?" he asked Kate.

"Oh, yes," she said, not wishing to seem impolite by getting directly to the purpose of their visit. "They tell me you are able to cure so many things."

"I try," he said modestly. "Fortunately, if I fail my patients can seek other physicians who will deplete their bodies with more drastic measures. It was not so for the Cherokees. If they failed, they failed. Today"—his eyes went to the iron pot he had simmering very slowly on the hearth—"I am working with yarrow leaves for poultices for spider bites. Do you have yarrow in your yard?"

"Oh, yes," said Kate, "and spiders, too."

"You should keep the ingredients for poultices handy. Here in the mountains we have many caves and many people who like to explore them." He looked at Edie and smiled. "Caves have few snakes—too chilly—but many spiders. I like to be ready."

They were all silent, even the little girls, sipping their tea. Edie, Kate realized, dreaded to hear what this man might have to tell them about Return. She delayed for her benefit.

"What are all these herbs you have hanging from the ceiling?"

He stood up and touched each dried bunch with pride. "Willow leaves for infusions for rheumatism, wormwood to revive a comatose patient, wild cherry to make a syrup for colds, peach leaves to combine with cornmeal to make a poultice for risings, tobacco to fry with elder leaves to kill the insects that infest the ears and dry up the brain."

The little girls shivered and Kate thought she might

have had enough, too, although there were dozens of other shriveled and sere plants hanging there.

The old gentleman, sensing their flagging interest, put down his cup and turned his chair to face them.

"It's Return you want to know about, isn't it?"

"Yes, sir, if you please," said Edie.

"I don't know," he said. "I can only tell you that he's deep in the ground. Bad, very bad."

"Where?" asked Edie desperately. "Tell us where."

"Can we save him?" asked Kate.

"You cannot. But make haste. He deserves a better grave. You will find him, I can't say where. Somewhere beyond Scratch Ankle Road. The other one, too. A spot very jeopardous."

"But we've been all up and down Scratch Ankle," protested Edie. "We've looked everywhere—everywhere!"

"Look again," whispered the old man. "Deep. Deep." He stood up by way of dismissal.

"Can't you tell us any more?" pleaded Edie. "Who hurt him?"

The old man reached up and pulled a shriveled leaf from a bunch in the ceiling and made no answer.

"The other man missing, a man named Banks. Can you tell us where he is?" asked Kate.

"Alive. In little trouble," said the old man.

"Let's go." Edie sighed, pushing her handkerchief into her mouth to keep from sobbing. "Jim and Smokey . . . let's get them. They'll keep trying," she said as she reached the car.

Kate and the girls hurried to get in, pausing only

briefly to thank Dr. Poultice, who offered them a limp hand and hardly seemed to pay attention to what they were saying.

"Would you say we learned anything?" Kate asked as they attained the road.

Edie shook her head. "Only what we knew. It's too late for Turn."

As they reached the paved road, the sheriff's car appeared. He forgot blue light and siren and flapped an arm out the open window to stop them. His young face looked stunned and more unhappy than ever.

"I need you, Edie," he said. "Lorena's dying. May not last the day. She should have somebody with her. Do you mind? I'll try to find some of her relatives. But in the meantime..."

"I'll go," Edie said promptly. "Here, Kate, take my car and get the food to Blue Hole. I'll ride with Jeff. See you back in town or the hospital... whatever... later."

"Sheriff!" Kate called suddenly. "Did you find somebody to stand guard outside Lorena's room at the hospital?"

For the first time the young sheriff's face lightened in a smile.

"Sure did," he said. "Your photographer. He didn't have to have a gun and a badge. He had his camera and he told anybody who tried to get in that they were violating the law and he would take their picture. Worked!"

What a wonderful use of Chris Mallory, Kate thought as she slid into the driver's seat and waited while the sheriff turned around and headed back to town.

By now she knew how to find Blue Hole and she

pushed the little Blazer to get there. It was well past mid-day and the searchers, if they had been depending on Edie's basket of food, would be starving. The tents brought by the legislators were still standing on the greensward that by now was mostly mud, and only one of the lawmakers remained. He sat on a camp stool glancing nervously at the water flowing into the Blue Hole and alternately at the sky.

Kate and the girls hauled the picnic basket and Thermos jug across the little footlog to his campsite.

"Hi, Mr. Hawkins," Kate said. "Are you keeping the campfires burning? Did you have a miserable night out here in the weather?"

"Not too bad for me," the representative said. "After we got down from the mountain I crawled in my sleeping bag and went to sleep. The other boys had a bad scare and took off. I haven't seen them since."

"What on earth?" asked Kate.

"Well, it was kind of funny," the legislator said sheepishly. "They were sitting by the campfire having a few drinks to ward off the cold and this . . . er . . . thing came up out of the hole and swum straight for them! It was all black and shiny with a mask over its face and I reckon they thought it was some creature from the black lagoon."

"And they ran off and left you?" Kate asked.

"Well, I was asleep and I don't wake easy. By the time I came to, the creature was standing here by our campfire warming himself. He was one of them cavers in a wet suit. I laughed a-plenty."

Kate laughed, too. "I bet that was scary."

The legislator wiped his eyes. "Spooky, but funny after the fellow explained it. You can't see it, but there's a stream over yonder flowing into the Blue Hole that comes out of a right big cave. The only way you can get to it from here is to swim, and the ceiling on the passage is so low you have to have scuba gear. Anybody would recognize that in daylight, but it was after midnight and raining and the firelight made it look eerie. That slick black suit, that mask."

"I'd a been sure 'nough scared," said Sheena, speaking for the first time.

"Not me," said Kim Sue. "I'd a shot him."

Representative Hawkins was eyeing the picnic basket hungrily.

"Oh, I'm sorry," said Kate. "Edie Putnam sent you and the others some lunch. There's coffee in the Thermos. She thought the cavers might be coming down off the mountain and she put in plenty of food. Why don't you go ahead and eat? And if you're here when they get back, you can share."

"I'll be here, I reckon. I have to wait for the state heli-copter to come back for us. And I should go on and break camp, looks like. They haven't found any sign of Turn or Motley Banks, have they? Don't seem much point in hanging around. Except"—he grinned ruefully—"how do you get away from here?"

"I could offer you a ride," Kate said, "but I planned to go back up to Scratch Ankle and look around a little more. Would you want to go along?"

"No, much obliged. I better wait here for the others, in case they get brave enough to come back."

Kate found Scratch Ankle without too much trouble. The upper end of the road was paved, with a few pretty houses and well-kept yards on either side. It seemed to have nothing to do with the sad trail the miners had known, especially those who had been mistreated convicts dragging their shackles and chains underground every day. Someone had told her there was a hill just off the road where convicts were buried. She decided to stop there first.

It was a good-sized cemetery with plain flat headstones which carried no names. Was it because the dead did not deserve the stigma of their names engraved in a convict cemetery? Or was it because those who had abused them did not care to go to the trouble and expense of markers? She wandered among them, pausing to admire, in a sheltered corner, a stand of blooming daffodils. Someone had cared enough to plant them there. She brooded sadly about the men, black and white, who had been victims of the vicious convict lease system. Even Scarlett's friends in *Gone With the Wind* had been horrified that she would use convict labor in her sawmill. The operators of the coal mines in these mountains had no such scruples.

Kate turned to show the girls the flowers and tell them something about the people who were buried there, but they were nowhere in sight. She walked to the Blazer, thinking they may have gotten back in. After all, children had little interest in cemeteries. They were not in the car.

She leaned in and blew the horn and then she started

calling their names. The woods around the cemetery were not particularly thick. The mountain slope behind it was only moderately steep. There was no dangerous cliff close by.

She walked to the back of the little graveyard, calling as she walked. There was a rustle in the bushes and Kim Sue appeared, crying.

Kate ran to meet her. "What's the matter? Where's Sheena? Where did you all go?"

"Miss Kate, somebody's in a big old well back there crying for help. Sheena was trying to poke a stick down for him to get hold of! I come to tell you!"

"Well, you shouldn't have wandered off. Now show me where Sheena is!"

"We didn't have time to tell you. We saw Smokey the Bear, and we wanted to catch up with him!"

"Oh, for goodness' sake!" snapped Kate. "You saw a shadow or something."

She was walking so fast Kim Sue had trouble keeping up with her. She was clawing at her blue-jeaned legs where heavy briars had taken hold.

"No, ma'am, it was Smokey the Bear. He had on the hat and the brown suit. He waved his paw at us to come on and then run into the forest. We wanted to catch up with him, but—"

"Never mind," said Kate. "Show me where Sheena is."

Down a briar-thick slope and up a hill, she saw the tall masonry coping of an air shaft, the kind that reaches deep into the coal mines. The rocks, laid in a beautiful pattern, made a tower twenty feet tall and eight or ten feet in circumference. She saw no sign of Sheena, but then she heard her.

"Shut up that hollering," she was saying to somebody deep within the shaft as she leaned through a rectangular opening on the side. "Miss Kate will git you out. So be quiet. You're gittin' on my nerves."

Kate pushed her out of the way and leaned into the window-sized opening near the base of the shaft. Daylight struck the upper half of it, illuminating walls covered with green moss and small ferns. At intervals narrow rock shelves projected from the sides, maybe enough to serve as steps if they weren't too slippery and the climber had a rope. She could not see anybody, but she called out anyhow.

"How far down are you? If I dropped a rope to you, could you climb out?"

"No! Arm broken!" a man's voice she didn't quite recognize answered.

"Are you at the bottom of the well?"

"No! Hanging on a tree branch. Halfway, maybe. For God's sake, hurry. I can't hang on much longer!"

Kate pulled her head out and squatted on the briar-thick well sweep. She needed a caver and it might be an hour before she could get anybody. These air shafts were very deep, she knew. She remembered hearing that some of them plunged seventy feet into the mines. Nobody could fall that far and live.

She stood up. "Girls, I want you to go out there on the paved road and stop anybody who comes along. If there are no cars passing, go as fast as you can to those houses

126

we passed back there about a mile and tell them we need help. I'm gon' get Edie's rappelling gear and go into that shaft."

"Miss Kate, you don't know how to rappel!" cried Sheena, grabbing her arm. The little girl was white and trembling, and Kate hugged her briefly and made herself smile reassuringly before striking out for the Blazer and Edie's gear.

"I'm like Brer Rabbit. Remember? He climbed a tree and he didn't know how. He did it because he was 'obleeged' to. Remember? Now, run!"

CHAPTER FOUR

KATE RAN THROUGH the little graveyard, sidestepping the tombstones when she could, but not slowing down. From the back of the Blazer she snatched the nylon bag with Edie's rappelling gear, then reached back in and grabbed the hard hat and plopped it on her head. She had no idea why she would need it, if indeed she was going to need it. The neatly coiled rope was the only thing she thought she understood, and that not too well. She had flunked knots in the Girl Scouts and the idea of tying one that would support her weight, much less the weight of whatever man clung to a tree branch in that pit, was the most frightening thing she had ever faced. The day was chilly, but sweat poured off her brow and her hands were wet as she fumbled with the bag's zipper.

The girls had made it through the graveyard and disappeared down the little dirt road, but there was only a remote chance they would find any passerby who would take seriously their plea for help.

And that man in the well . . . Kate wished it would be Return, still able to cling to a fallen tree trunk and ask for help. But Banks, poor fellow—had he stumbled in while searching for Turn? It didn't seem likely that you could accidentally pitch into that shaft, but how else would he have gotten in there?

These thoughts raced through Kate's head as she galloped back through the graveyard, out of breath and unsteady on her legs. She was a walker, not a runner, especially with a hard hat banging about her ears and a bag full of rope and little metal thingamajigs bumping against her knees.

Oh, let him hang on till I get there, she prayed. *Keep that tree branch strong enough to hold him!*

The sun had moved when she got back to the shaft and the interior was not as light. She could make out the edges of the rock protruding along the sides near the top, but she couldn't see the human being below.

"Are you there?" she called into the shaft.

"Help! Help me!" cried a weak voice.

"Help is here," said Kate with what she recognized as insane confidence. "Hang on, I'm coming!"

She knew nothing about rappelling except what she had heard Edie explaining to the girls, but she knew she had to do something. No human being could be allowed to plunge to his death if a rope tied to a tree would save him.

Her hands trembled as she unwound two neatly coiled ropes. She looked around for a tree to tie them to. Two trees, Edie had said. But there was only one tree close by and it was a small cedar. Would it hold? It had to, she decided. The rope wouldn't extend up the hill to the old broad-beamed oak there, which was what she needed.

She quickly wrapped one of the two ropes around the broadest part of the cedar trunk and tied it with many knots, none they had tried to teach her in Girl Scouts but the only ones she knew—from tying shoestrings or Christmas packages or affixing a new piece of yarn to her knitting. Grabbing the free end of the rope, she ran to the window in the rock coping and called down.

"I'm dropping you a rope! Can you grab it and hold on till I get there?"

For response she got a faint moan.

If only she could see, but the lights Edie had—a bunch of them, because she never entered a cave without at least three—were back in the Blazer. She dared not make that run across the graveyard again—the man in the shaft might not last, and she wasn't sure her own legs were up to it. If only the sun had stayed put. It had given plenty of light when she first peered down into that hole in the ground.

Now only the first few feet of damp and mossy wall were visible.

She spread the second rope out on the ground. The seat sling she recognized. The rest she wasn't sure about. Steel rings—maybe to attach the seat? Swiftly, because she didn't know what else to do, she wrapped the rope around her waist and between her legs and then around each leg separately, tying everything together with lumpy, cumbersome knots. She was glad the girls weren't there to see her. They had paid attention when Edie explained the gear. She had only half listened and like everything else in her life, she reflected, what she had not learned was what she needed.

Within moments she had built herself a cage of rope and taken a seat on the ground beside the little opening. All she had to do was slide into the pit, and suddenly her resolution failed her. She hated dark holes in the ground. She was terrified that the rocks jutting from the wall harbored snakes. She had no hope that the snarl of rope would hold her. And if she had misjudged the distance to the injured man, she would probably go catapulting to the bottom of the shaft. She had no way of judging how far she had to go to reach him, and so she guessed—as many feet, she supposed, as the distance from her back door to the little log corncrib at the edge of her garden. Twenty feet? Thirty feet?

Hopefully, she called to the man.

"Did you get the rope? Are you holding on?"

There was no answer.

If only he had grabbed the rope and somehow wound it around himself, but he said he had a broken arm and if he had been hanging there in the shaft long, he was probably too weak and dazed to help himself.

Before she made herself swing out into the hole, Kate took a look around. Maybe the girls had found help and she wouldn't have to go down there. Already her hands on the rope hurt and she remembered Edie wore heavy gloves.

Well, she couldn't get out now and go look for them.

This was one case when you couldn't say, *Excuse me, I forgot my gloves.*

There was a noise in the shaft, a creaking like cracking wood. The tree branch he held to!

"Hang on!" Kate called. "I'm coming!"

She knew that rappellers had ways of pacing themselves, dropping slowly a little at the time. She supposed it was done by hanging onto the rope and sliding gradually. She made a loop around her wrist and as she eased into the shaft, it pulled tight.

Wrong, she thought. *It'll pull my arm out of its socket.* Clutching at a rock on the shaft wall, she disentangled her wrist. If only she knew how to play out the rope gradually . . . if only somebody would come and get her out of that hole! Holding tight to the first thing her hand found, she made a decision. She would not rappel. She would emulate old-time well diggers in the country who dug themselves toeholds in the clay walls and ascended and descended like they were on a ladder. She would not swing free but would hang on to the rocks and set her feet onto those rocky shelves one at the time and not even think about snakes. Edie had boots. She herself wore sneakers, slippery on the bottom and low-cut. If only . . .

I won't think, she told herself firmly. *I'll just do it.*

"Hang on!" she called into the shaft. "I'm coming!"

Everything she touched was slippery and twice her feet slipped off the rocks and she swung free into the shaft, hanging on only by gripping the rope with both hands, which by now were bruised and bleeding. Her eyes didn't seem to get accustomed to the darkness, as she had hoped, but she could see far, far below the shimmer of water and silhouetted against it a human body crumpled across a heavy tree branch which could have blown into the shaft or pushed through the rock coping or the earth below it. Was it breaking? How was it supported? She dared not think about it. All she had strength for was to brace herself against the slick wall with one hand, hold on to the rope with the other, and put one foot at a time on the next lower jutting rock. She prayed the toeholds would last. If the rocks started slipping out, she and the man below her had no hope of climbing out.

Kate had no idea how they would get out. She had not thought beyond saving him from falling. She supposed something would occur to her when she got there. Rappellers and cavers got people out of hazardous places all the time. If the victims were dead, it was called "body recovery."

Oh, don't let this one be dead, she prayed as she alternately pushed her feet into the niches along the wall and fought to keep from swinging free and falling.

Suddenly she was there! Her foot struck something soft. The tendency of the rope to carry her downward was halted.

"Oohh!" moaned a voice. "You're standing on my arm. It's broken! Ooohh!"

"Sorry," said Kate, trying to pull herself a little to the side by clutching at the rope and bracing herself against the wall. She was afraid the tree trunk wasn't strong enough to hold them both, but as long as she could hang on to it she wouldn't fall any farther.

"I'm gon' see if I can help you," she said to the lump beside her. He smelled of whiskey and cigars and fear and she couldn't see his face, but it didn't matter.

"Did you get that rope I threw down?"

"Yeah, but I can't tie it. Only one hand—and that's holding on."

"Okay," said Kate. "I think I can loop it around you and tie it so you won't fall all the way."

"Who are you?" the voice asked.

"Hush, now, and let me think. Try to raise up a little bit so I can get this thing around you." Then, as an afterthought, "I'm Kate Mulcay."

"Oh, God," moaned the man. "Wasn't there anybody else that could come?"

"No," said Kate. "We got to make do. Who are you?"

"PawPaw," he croaked. And then, quaveringly, "Don't . . . let . . . me . . . fall!"

"We both may fall if you don't shut up and lie still," Kate said grimly. And to herself she thought, *It's true. I can't get him or myself out of here. And he may try to kill me again if he's the one who shot at me.*

Sheena and Kim Sue stood by the paved road long moments before a car came by. They waved frantically and the people in the car waved back and drove on.

"Miss Kate said if no cars come to start walking toward them houses we saw," Sheena said. "You go. I got a better idea. I'm going back to the Blazer."

"Sheena, you cain't drive airy car!" cried Kim Sue. "You know you cain't. Them cliffs and curves! You know you cain't!"

"Hush up and listen," said Sheena. "I ain't gon' try to drive. I think Miss Edie's got a CB in there. I'm gon' holler for help. But just in case, you keep a-going and stop somebody, if you have to jump in the road."

Kim Sue burst into tears.

Sheena viewed her without compassion. "That's good. Keep a-bawling," she said. "Anybody seeing you cry will stop to help. But run! Run fast as you can!"

She turned and loped down the cemetery road, thinking all the time that maybe it wasn't a CB radio she saw in Miss Edie's van. Maybe it was a weather radio or something like that. People in the mountains seemed crazy about the weather. If there was no CB, she knew what she would have to do, in spite of what Kim Sue said and what she herself knew. She couldn't drive airy car, but like Miss Kate said about going in that hole, maybe she'd be obleeged to.

The Blazer was not locked and the key was in the ignition. Just like Miss Kate, Sheena thought disapprovingly. Never locked nothing. Never thought anybody would do her bad—and look at her now, in the bottom of a mine. Sheena got in the car and turned on the switch. There was a CB! Her young heart lifted.

She grabbed it with both hands and pressed the button she had learned about years before when CB radios were the rage and two of her truck-driving uncles had let the children play with them.

"Breaker! Breaker!" she yelled. "Anybody! Anybody anywhere! I need help! Miss Kate's in the air shaft. Help! Somebody help us!" And then she burst into tears.

"Little girl, are you playing?" a querulous old voice asked. "Because it's against the law to play with these radios!"

Sheena responded by wailing, "We need help! We need the sheriff! Oh, somebody please come before Miss Kate gits kilt in the air shaft!"

She leaned into the windshield, looking at the contraption in her hand. Had she pushed the button for sending or the one for receiving? She couldn't remember, so she did it all over again.

"Child," a weak voice said, "punch nine. That's the emergency channel."

Sheena obediently punched nine and shouted, "Help! This is Sheena and Miss Kate's in the well! She'll die. Somebody come quick!" The radio crackled and several voices spoke at once. One of them she recognized as the sheriff's.

"Sheena, this is Sheriff Atkins," he said. And the other voices were suddenly silent. "Tell me what your trouble is and where you are!"

"My trouble is Miss Kate going in that big well where a man is. She went to get him out. And Sheriff . . . " she started crying again, "Miss Kate don't know how to rappel!"

"I know, honey," said the sheriff soothingly. "Tell me which big well."

"The one by the convict cemetery."

"Near Scratch Ankle Road?" another voice put in.

"Un-huh," said Sheena uncertainly. "I think."

"Sheena," said the sheriff. "Hang on and don't worry. We'll be there to get Miss Kate out in a few minutes."

Sheena put the hand-held microphone down on the seat and started across the cemetery. Then she turned back and picked it up and pushed the button.

"Ten Four, good buddy," she said in the timeless patois of CBers.

By the time Sheena had crossed the cemetery and was approaching the big air shaft, pickup trucks had started arriving from all directions; six cavers who had been close by on the mountain, wearing walkie-talkies, had gotten the word and passed it along. They were there with their ropes and lights, striding confidently across the field in sturdy boots and with well-gloved hands.

Sheena saw them and suddenly remembered Kim Sue.

"My little sister," she quavered. "Did anybody see her on the road?"

"Don't tell me your sister is in the air shaft too!" snapped a caver.

"No, sir," said Sheena humbly. "She went down the paved road looking for help. She ain't but eleven year old."

At that moment the sheriff wheeled up, his blue dome light whirling. Kim Sue was with him.

Sheena rushed to her side and, lest somebody think she loved her sister and had worried about her, she said accusingly, "Ain't Mommer told you not to ride with strange men?"

Kim Sue got out of the car, her jeans mud-stained at the knee, where she had stumbled and fallen in the road, her face tear-smudged and dirty. She lifted her chin and said loftily, "The sheriff ain't strange."

Kate was lifted out of the shaft first, to make room for one of the cavers who was a doctor to go down with splints and bandages and painkiller to prepare the injured man to be moved. Somebody had wrapped Kate in a blanket and handed her a cup of coffee and she sat on the ground, leaning against a rock, and watched the rescue operation. The Gandy sisters crawled as close to her as they could get. One of them held one of her rope-burned, rock-cut hands, which somebody had smeared with ointment and bandaged. The other dug a chin into her shoulder. She smiled at them, but her mind was busy trying to retrieve some detail she had seen. She had been so engrossed with that slippery rope and those knots, she hadn't paid enough attention.

Suddenly she knew what she had seen. Blood.

There were smears of dark brown blood on rocks near the top of the shaft. Her hands, although cut, had not bled that much. Besides, fresh blood was red, not brown. PawPaw? She didn't think a broken arm bled.

She called to the sheriff.

He had been standing by, watching the cavers work, but he came to her side.

"You okay, Kate?"

"All right, but Sheriff, I think Turn Pickett is at the bottom of the well!"

The sheriff turned swiftly and called Smokey.

Within minutes a floodlight was rigged up and Smokey himself waited to descend to the bottom of the shaft.

The girls stirred restlessly against her, and Kim Sue, her chin in Kate's shoulder, whispered, "What happened to Smokey the Bear? We saw him. We really did, Miss Kate."

Kate threw off the blanket and stood up. Horace Waters, a Georgia Bureau of Investigation agent she had met years before on a serial murder case in Columbus, was standing by the sheriff and she went over and touched him on the shoulder. He turned to greet her, but she brushed aside cordiality to whisper urgently.

"A man wearing one of those state patrol Sergeant York hats, looking like Smokey the Bear, was here a few minutes before I got here. My girls saw him and he ran off into the woods. He beckoned to them to follow him, but they heard the groans in the well and didn't go."

"Oh, good God!" he said. "A child molester."

"Almost as bad," Kate said. "A murderer."

The sheriff crouched over the side of the well and stared in disbelief as the makeshift gurney swung to the surface bearing the mud-stained groaning hulk that was PawPaw. In the excitement of her own rescue, Kate had not thought to mention the identity of the man halfway down the shaft. The sheriff was slow to believe that stout, potbellied PawPaw, the town's richest man, was a victim. As they wrapped PawPaw in a blanket and prepared to put him in the rescue vehicle, the young sheriff stuck by his side.

"Who did it, PawPaw?" he asked. "Who put you in the shaft?"

PawPaw closed his eyes and shook his head.

The caver who was a doctor checked the splint he had contrived below ground and said, "Better take him in to the emergency room, Sheriff, and talk to him later."

"Go ahead," the sheriff said, diverted by a muffled shout from the bottom of the shaft.

"Here!" called Jim hoarsely. "Body! It's Turn!"

There was no need to ask if he was alive. They all knew he couldn't have survived both the bloody struggle and the fall, much less twenty-four hours of exposure. So the business of body retrieval began.

Kate didn't want the girls to be there when poor Turn's tortured body reached the surface. She murmured to the sheriff that she was taking Edie's car back to her and needed to call the newspaper.

The girls walked along beside her, sedate and subdued. The afternoon's experience had drained them as well as Kate herself. Before they reached the Blazer, Sheena said hesitantly, "Miss Kate. It may not start. I think I forgot and left the switch on."

Kate looked at the troubled little face and smiled reassuringly. "Plenty of people here to jump us off, if need be," she said. "What you did, what you both did"—she looked at the drying tear paths on Kim Sue's dirty face—

"was perfectly wonderful! You were smart to think of it. I should have remembered the CB and saved myself the trip down in that hole."

"Was you skeered down there?" asked Kim Sue.

"Oh, yeah," said Kate cheerfully. "I was plenty scared. I'd never done anything like that before. We've got to get lessons, all three of us. Might come in handy someday when somebody else needs help."

The young faces brightened. "We could start tomorrow," offered Sheena.

"Yeah!" put in Kim Sue. "I'll learn to fly off that mountain like a big old red-tailed hawk!" She stretched her arms and loped ahead, giving an imitation of a red-tailed hawk in full flight.

"I hate to put a damper on your spirits," said Kate, "but we've got to get you back home. School tomorrow."

"Sez you," said Sheena. "Teacher's workday. We got a holiday."

"We gon' stay and hep you ketch a killer," said Kim Sue.

Kate sighed—she didn't know whether from relief at not having to drive back to Atlanta tonight or at the prospect of the unalloyed presence of two such aides. They were capricious about taking orders. They were incorrigible about wandering off on their own.

Their wandering, she suddenly remembered, was what found PawPaw and the big hole in the ground. She hadn't planned to go that way, but they went in pursuit of a man dressed like Smokey the Bear, and they heard the cries for help from the air shaft.

Instead of scolding them for Sheena's impertinent "Sez you," she hugged them and opened the door to the Blazer. The switch was still on, but by a miracle it had not drained the battery. Perhaps they had not been gone as long as Kate felt. Seeping fatigue seemed to start in the bottoms of her sore feet and rise up in her body, making her arms and shoulders ache and feel limp. Her hands, burned by the rope and cut by the rocks, really hurt. She couldn't complain to Edie because she didn't feel like a lecture on proper preparation. Where were your gloves?

Where would Edie be anyhow? Hospital? Home? And what of poor Lorena? She stopped at the sheriff's office to use the phone. Luckily, Chris the photographer was there, again ensconced in the sheriff's chair with his feet on the sheriff's desk.

"Hi, babe," he greeted Kate and the girls cordially. "Where you been?"

"Down in a hole in the ground trying to help a man who was thrown down there," said Kate sourly. "Did you get pictures?"

"Well, not of that," said the young man defensively. "Nobody told me. They had me doing guard duty at the hospital for that old broad, Lorena. I stood 'em off, too, until her cousin or aunt or somebody took over."

"Are you sure they were her relatives and not somebody who might hurt her? Did Edie see them? Where is Edie?"

"They called her to the hospital office to make financial arrangements. You know how they are: Where's the

143

money coming from? While she was there Lorena's Aunt Somebody showed up—old biddy with a walking stick and a weird hat you wouldn't believe."

"Did you get a picture of her?"

"As a matter of fact"—he looked chagrined—"I didn't. She said she was of a religion that was against pictures, believed the devil would get you if you let your likeness be committed to film. I said what the hell and let her go on in."

Kate grabbed the phone and called the hospital. She asked for the administrator and found Edie in his office crying.

"Lorena . . ." she said in a queer strained voice. "They called me out of the room and . . . cut her throat! She's dying! I heard her scream! Oh, Kate!"

Kate ran for Edie's car where the Gandeys waited and raced to the hospital. Chris followed and got out of the staff car with his camera in hand, for once looking chastened. At the same time, an ambulance was pulling in to the emergency entrance with PawPaw. The sheriff followed.

Lorena was dead. A doctor and a nurse escorted Kate and the sheriff into a little waiting room, where Edie and her mother sat silent and blank-faced. Kate recognized the room as one of those little parlors hospitals reserve for grieving families, a place to put them when the shock of a loved one's death was fresh on them and they were likely to make noises of grief or outraged suggestions that the hospital was somehow to blame, all upsetting to staff

and other patients. Close a door on them and call it privacy. But where was Lorena's family?

"I couldn't find anybody kin to her around here," the
sheriff said.

"I think the last of her aunts died last year," offered
Mrs. Putnam.

"But what about the woman who came to see her? She
told Chris, our photographer, she was an aunt."

The moment she said it, Kate knew it was a false
assumption. The person with the walking stick and the
weird hat . . . where did she go? Who had seen her besides
Chris?

CHAPTER FIVE

THE SAME AMBULANCE that brought PawPaw to the hospital apparently brought the body of Turn Pickett in a plastic bag, and forensic experts from the state crime lab in Atlanta were at the back door to meet it.

Edie started for the stairs and her mother rose to follow her.

The young hospital administrator threw Kate an agonized look. "Don't let her . . ." he began. "It's not . . . She shouldn't see him yet. Can you stop her?"

Kate stopped both Edie and her mother on the stairs. "Let's wait," she said, taking hold of each of them by the arm. "Let's give them time for their examination—the crime lab people. Then—"

"Then we'll see him, honey," Mrs. Putnam said gently. "Plenty of time."

Ah, yes, Kate thought to herself. Plenty of time for Turn, for whom time had stopped, and plenty of time for no telling how many more murders in this serene little valley. She had already seen the cart go toward the elevator bearing the body of Lorena covered by not one but several sheets to cover the scarlet tide of the poor woman's blood. Whatever the hospital used to stanch the blood had not been effective until death itself dammed the red stream.

Edie, white-faced and trembling, turned back and her mother guided her toward the elevator. "We'll go home," she murmured to Kate. "That'll be best, won't it?"

Kate nodded. "I'll see you all later."

"Look, chick, I want to go home, too," said Chris, appearing suddenly in the stairwell. "I'm sick." He retched.

His face was in fact pale green and his golden hair was dark with sweat. For a second Kate wondered if murder was reaching out and touching her photographer friend.

"What happened?" Before he could answer, she knew. "You didn't try to get a picture of Lorena, did you?"

He nodded mutely. "They left the room and—"

"Aw, Chris," Kate said sympathetically, "you know we don't use pictures of dead bodies, especially mutilated ones."

He gulped. "I got both of them, Pickett and Lorena, and the man that was down in the well, too. Kate, I've had it! There are some rooms available at the Big Rock Motel. People start checking out on Sunday. Somebody called while I was in the sheriff's office and I told them we'd take them. You mind if I hole up there for a little while?"

Kate couldn't think of anything else he could do if he

had gotten a good picture of PawPaw. The mining shaft might make a good one, but clearly he was in no condition to go looking for it, if he was vomiting.

"Go ahead," she said. "Tell the motel people I'll take the other room and be checking in later."

She wanted to see PawPaw, but he was sitting in the sheriff's car surrounded by reporters and television crews. His arm was in a cast and there were patches of tape and bandage over his face and neck. He was plainly refusing to answer questions.

Kate decided to hold back till her competitors had given up and she could get the help of the sheriff for a quiet exclusive interview with PawPaw. After all, she had risked her life—butt, anyhow—to get him out of that well. He owed her some answers.

Meanwhile, Sheena and Kim Sue had gone to sleep on the waiting room sofa. Sleeping, they wouldn't be a nuisance, Kate thought, but she really should get them home. With all the people she needed to talk to, all the things she wanted to follow up, she didn't need even such peerless help as the Gandy sisters. She took the phone to the corner farthest from the sofa sleepers and dialed the Gandys' home as quietly as possible.

Their mother answered.

"Lordamercy, Kate!" she cried. "I'm glad you called!"

"Did the baby come?" Kate asked out of politeness.

"By the hardest," Mrs. Gandy said. "A fine baby girl, weighed nine pounds. Her water broke about ten o'clock and..."

Kate sighed. The last thing she wanted was a blow-by-blow account of the delivery. Country women of the old school, before the city came out to give them something else to think about, savored the details of birth and left no fecund particular unexplored.

To sidetrack Mommer, she asked the new baby's name.

Mrs. Gandy laughed proudly. "My sister's got a hand for names," she said. "She named Sheena and Kim Sue for me, did you know that? Well, I let her because I didn't know she was gon' keep on having young'uns of her own to name. She come up with a good one this time: Michael Madonna!"

"Oh, my," murmured Kate, choking a little. "Goodness."

"A name like that stands for something, you know," young Mrs. Gandy said ponderously.

"It does?" said Kate, and then hastily, "It does! Well, I know the girls are going to be thrilled to see their new cousin, and since we have run into some problems up here on Lookout Mountain and I'm gon' have to stay over awhile, I wonder if you could come and get them? I'll give you directions."

"Oh, Kate, I ain't got no way!" Mrs. Gandy said. "You know his car is on the blink." (Kate noted that she never called her husband by his name but simply "he-him-his," as if he were the only man in the world.) "And mine"— she giggled—"while I was at my sister's he drove it to the VFW club and . . . well, he took on . . . " Kate joined her in finishing it: "a little too much." She knew the rest. He wrecked it.

"Well, yes. Pretty bad. So we ain't got no way. Just let

the girls stay with you. I read in this morning's paper that you was involved in a murder and I told him, 'Lord, the girls will be tickled with that.'"

Kate made sounds of resignation and hung up. The Gandys spoke of murder as if it were something designed for the edification of the young. She wanted to cry, *Why don't you get ballet lessons for them or enroll them in aerobics?* Fools, she raged inwardly, to turn their fragile offspring over to an old police reporter!

But the fragile offspring were stirring on the hospital's sofa and they threw such beatific smiles at Kate that she felt her annoyance melting. In spite of fools for parents, they were remarkably nice, smart children and she would think of something to do with them while she worked. She remembered the Big Rock Motel. Television! That would occupy them for hours.

On the way out of the hospital Kate paused to see if PawPaw and the sheriff were still at the ambulance entrance. They had gone and so had the covey of reporters and photographers from other papers and television stations.

She would drop by the sheriff's office and see if PawPaw had told him anything that would solve the deaths of Turn and Lorena and at least explain the attempt on herself.

The sheriff wasn't just noncommittal. He was uninformed.

"Kate, he was the most shut-mouthed, say-nothing

feller that's ever been in this office—at least since I been here," he said.

Kate smiled, figuring he had been there roughly a month. Not a Guinness record for shut-mouth, say-nothing, to say the least.

"First, may I use your phone? I need to call the office," she said.

The sheriff nodded, then stood up and walked to the window so she could use his desk and chair. The details of Lorena's death were easy to dictate and the retrieval of Representative Pickett's body she could handle in a few brief paragraphs, but the presence of PawPaw in the well and her own part in it gave her trouble. If she described her rescue effort, she would be making some kind of heroine of herself and that was not allowed. The newspaper frowned on valor in staffers. Sometimes they unwittingly committed it, as Kate herself had done with Paw-Paw, but it was considered self-serving to put it in the paper.

The rewrite man, a veteran who was good at his job, helped her muddle through. She hung up the phone and turned back to the sheriff.

"Well, where is he? PawPaw, I mean. Maybe I could talk to him. After all—"

"Yeah," said the sheriff, suddenly seeing the point she was going to try not to make. "He sure ought to talk to you! If it hadn't been for you, he'd be in the bottom of that shaft—dead. That was mighty nice of you, Kate, to go down there and keep a hold on him till help came."

Kate smiled at the embroidered-doily, tea-party word

"nice." She hadn't been "nice"; she'd been dirty and incompetent and scared. But if the sheriff was paying her a useful compliment, she would accept it.

"Where did you say he is?"

"Oh, he wanted to go home and go to bed and there was no way I could keep him. It's not against the law to fall in a well."

"Did he fall or was he pushed?"

The sheriff, back in his swivel chair, looked out the window. "That I don't know."

"How about Lorena? Did he know who killed her?"

The young sheriff looked at her wearily. "Said he didn't."

"Did he shoot at me?"

The sheriff looked surprised and then chagrined. "Kate, so much has happened I plumb forgot to ask him. But I don't think he would have done that to Lorena—I think whoever shot at you thought you was her—and we know he didn't cut her throat. He wasn't hardly out of the well when that happened."

"Well, who did? Did you find any prints or the murder weapon?"

"Not the sign of one. Of course, the boys from the crime lab might come up with something. They gon' take over on PawPaw when they get through with Turn and the fingerprints at the air shaft and all like that. They told me they wanted the clothes he was wearing for testing and he promised me soon as he got home he would change and put them in a plastic bag."

"And the murder weapon?"

"Knives. Some kind of thin-bladed knife that would be easy to hide coming into the hospital. Of course, an ax would have worked at Turn's trailer."

Kate sighed and stood up.

"How about Representative Banks? Any word on him?"

The sheriff stood up. "Kate, you're a gadfly, showing me my duty. I forgot about Banks. I'll go now and see if there's any word at the Blue Hole. Why don't you . . ." He looked at her muddy, moss-stained, blood-spotted clothes and smiled. "Why don't you go somewhere and get a bath?"

"Sure, Sheriff," she said crisply. "I'll get out of your hair. I think I have a room at the Big Rock Motel. Call me there if you decide to let the press in on your investigation."

For once the sheriff was decisive. "I'll do that, Kate," he said, walking her toward the door.

On the way to the Big Rock, Kate looked at her slacks and shirt and the clothes of the girls and shuddered. It would be wonderful if the motel provided a washer-dryer and she could do a spot of laundry for herself and the girls while she took a nap. But mindful of the unanswered questions that were piling up, she decided not to count on it. If need be she would seek out Mrs. Armentrout's Wal-Mart and buy a change of clothes.

Dusk was settling in as she drove into the Big Rock parking lot, a very ugly flat-topped yellow brick structure. With the plentiful native materials, beautiful stone, and timber, it could have been more inviting, Kate thought.

But it was laid out in the usual rectangle, with no trees and with empty concrete flower boxes, ornamented occasionally with paper cups from Shoney's restaurant. However, the elderly woman at the desk was decorative enough in her David Dow tweed suit and pearls with smoothly coiffed white hair and pink cheeks. And she was welcoming.

"We've had a swift turnover this weekend," she said. "Conventioneers. They came, complained loudly and constantly, left their rooms in a hurrah's nest, and checked out, taking our best towels with them," she said good-humoredly, as if sharing a joke with Kate and the girls. "And I'm temporary manager, Mrs. Charles Land."

"Oh, we won't do nothing like that, ma'am," said Sheena earnestly.

"I know you won't," the woman said. "I know who Kate Mulcay is and I am very glad to have you all here in my motel. It's not really mine. I just work here, but I do like a nice clientele."

Kate, signing the register, knew the girls were considering that word, "clientele," and she was back to "nice." People did expect you to be nice in this funny, murder-assailed county, she thought.

"The rooms do have telephones?" she asked.

"And teevees?" put in Kim Sue.

"Both," said the proprietor. And looking at their dirty faces and clothes, she added, "*And* hot water and soap!"

Kate laughed. "We need it. Unfortunately, we didn't come prepared to stay and we didn't bring enough clothes.

When the stores open we might go find something."

"Murder is always so sudden, isn't it?" Mrs. Land said reflectively.

Kate looked at her in surprise. This elegant lady in her fine clothes didn't seem to be a person who would be privy to violence and homicide.

"Oh, you've read about it," Kate said, wondering if she could pick up an afternoon newspaper somewhere there in the lobby.

"Yes, but I expected it was going to come to that," Mrs. Land said, handing Kate a key. "I could almost have predicted that young Return Pickett would meet an untimely end."

Before Kate could pursue that line, Mrs. Land reached behind her and took a coat off a coatrack. "I see my family is here to gather me up," she said. "I'll probably see you tomorrow. The regular manager, Mr. Goodman, will be here shortly and if you need anything call him. Have a pleasant night."

Gracefully, moving swiftly on her pretty high-heeled pumps and leaving behind a whiff of some expensive fragrance, Mrs. Land was gone.

Thoughtfully, Kate picked up the room key and led the girls down the outside walk beside the building to their room. The room was clean with its plastic-shrouded glasses and tape across the toilet, but no more cheerful than any modern motel swathed in chocolate-colored draperies with matching bedspreads and carpet. Kate thought fleetingly that as far as decor was concerned, she preferred Addie Armentrout's "Home in the Pines." The little silver cabin at least had a woodstove, and it would have been cheerful to sit by it on a winter night if you weren't out looking for murderers. She ran the girls through the shower and took a slow soak herself. Before she set off for Edie's, she settled them in front of the television.

"You stay in this room," she said. "Keep the door locked and if anybody asks for me—or your mother or any other grown-up—say, 'She's outside, she'll be back in a minute.' Don't let anybody inside. I'm going to run over to Miss Edie's and exchange cars with her and get our bags. I'll be right back before you've even looked at one program."

The novelty of motel television pleased the girls, and they waved Kate off with newly scrubbed paws.

"If you see any food . . ." began Sheena tentatively.

"Oh, my goodness!" Kate turned at the door and looked at them. "I forgot. You haven't had anything since dinner at Mrs. Putnam's. How about hamburgers and milkshakes?"

Their smiles assured her it would be acceptable fare.

"I'll be right back!"

Outside the door Kate thought of Chris and wondered if he had recovered sufficiently to eat something and talk to her. The company car was not in that area of the parking lot, but he might have stowed it somewhere in the back. She stopped by the motel office to get his room number.

The office was empty, the front desk unmanned. There was a little bell by the cash register and she punched it.

Nothing happened, and after a few minutes she rang the bell again. Down the hallway back of the desk a door opened and a tall, heavyset man came lumbering out, digging at his eyes with his fingers and stumbling blindly. He had a frowsy beard and long uncombed hair and he wore a dirty shirt, its tails hanging loosely over khaki pants.

"Whatcha want?" he said brusquely.

"I'm Mrs. Mulcay," Kate said stiffly, suddenly needing to be formal. "I'm looking for my associate, Mr. Christopher Mallory. Will you give me his room number, please."

The man yawned, scratched his belly, and stood looking at her with a grin on his face.

"You that newspaper woman, ain't you?"

"Yes," Kate said.

"Well, you all know so much down in Atlanta, always running everybody's business. You ought to know we can't give out room numbers of our guests. They may not want to be bothered by company barging in. Besides," he leered, "this ain't the kind of motel that has women going to the rooms of men."

Kate fought an impulse to reach across the desk and slap his face. Instead, she said pleasantly, "Oh, you mean it's not a whorehouse? Well, in that case I'll just phone him." She reached for the phone on the desk but he came out of his lethargy and grabbed it first.

"Pay station outside," he said. "This here is a business phone."

Angrily Kate stalked out the door, digging into her bag for a quarter. In front of the plastic pay phone shell on the side of the building she paused. Mrs. Land had said her relief at the front desk would be a Mr. Goodman. Kate smiled.

Expecting the oaf to bark an answer into the motel phone, she was startled when he said in a mincing falsetto, "Big Rock Moo-tell!"

"Mr. Goodman," she said softly, "please ring Chris Mallory's room . . . or I'm gon' tell your daddy, the distinguished legislator!"

He coughed and cleared his throat—or was he retching? Then he said squeakily, "That's room 275. I'll ring."

The room didn't answer and Kate turned from the phone thoughtfully. Chris might be out looking for food and she should get on to a take-out window, but Mr. Goodman . . . could it be that he was the flowery oratorical lawmaker's son? Such a slob? The khaki pants . . . surely he wasn't a military type. More likely a hunter.

She gave up and hurried to McDonald's to stock up on cheeseburgers and chocolate milkshakes for the girls. There was nothing that she could think of for herself after what her digestive system had been through that day. She settled for a cup of coffee to go and hurried back to the motel.

"Don't eat in bed," she admonished the girls, and then she withdrew the order. Crumbs and grease on the dark brown, cigarette-smelling bedspreads wouldn't make much difference.

The Putnams' house was dark except for a light in the kitchen. Kate parked on the street and went to the front door. She could hear the doorbell resounding in the back of the house, but it was a long time before Mrs. Putnam came to the door. Even as she opened it and invited her in, Kate heard the back door closing and a car start up in the backyard.

Mrs. Putnam looked flustered.

"Come in, dear," she said. "Sit down. Edie isn't here. She went out to the Blue Hole with some of the cavers."

"Oh, I can't stay," Kate said. "I left the girls at the Big Rock Motel. We got a room there and we won't impose on your hospitality tonight. I just thought..."

A car was coming down the driveway out of the back-yard. She couldn't see any headlights. On impulse she ran to the door and looked out. The porch light caught the driver in its beam. PawPaw and somebody else. Kate couldn't see who before the big Lincoln picked up speed and turned into the street.

Kate watched its taillights disappear in the distance before she moved back toward the living room.

Mrs. Putnam waited impassively.

"You're curious about my other guests," she said stonily.

Kate studied the pink face under the soft gray hair. Something had happened to the "nice" Mrs. Putnam, maker of brownies, washer of clothes, source of comfort and gracious hospitality.

"I don't know," she said uncertainly. "I've been looking for PawPaw. I wish I had known he was here. I need to talk to him."

"Your bags are in the hall," Mrs. Putnam said.

"What?" Kate said. And then, "Oh, thank you." She

started toward the two little nylon zipper bags by the guest-room door and turned suddenly. "Mrs. Putnam, something is wrong. Tell me what it is. I can't go with you acting so angry and mysterious. Why was PawPaw here? Who was that with him? What's going on?"

Mrs. Putnam attempted a smile that didn't come off.

"I think you'd better get back to the little girls," she said. "Our nice little town is brimming with evil. You don't want to leave them alone too long."

She had struck a sensitive chord. Kate felt a sudden compulsion to get out of this pleasant comfortable house and back to Sheena and Kim Sue before something did happen to them. She grabbed the bags and strode to the door.

"Your key is in your car," Mrs. Putnam called after her. "Leave Edie's on the table there."

Kate looked back at her and surprised a look of pain on her face.

Chris was taking his camera out of his car in front of his motel room when Kate got back to the Big Rock.

"Where you been?" asked Kate. "Feeling better?"

"Aw, I'm okay," he said. "Ran over to Chattanooga to transmit my pictures."

"Good," said Kate, unlocking the door to her room and looking at the girls, both of them safely asleep on top of the ugly bedspreads, chocolate-shake smears on their faces.

She closed the door and turned back to the photographer. "I need to talk to you," she said.

"My place or yours?" He strove for jocularity.

"Yours," said Kate shortly. "I don't want to wake up the girls."

He unlocked his door and held it open for her.

"Tell me," Kate said, taking a seat in the chair by the window, "what did that person who claimed to be Lorena's aunt look like?"

"Well, she wasn't Jackie Onassis," said Chris. "Tall, hefty. The southern word: tacky."

"Are you sure it was a woman?"

Chris, sitting on one of the beds, turned restively. "No, I'm not sure. I'm not sure at all. I did think her voice was kind of hoarse for a woman's, but she had that walking stick and I figured the old biddy might have been down sick with something."

"Walking stick," Kate said thoughtfully. "Walking stick! Chris, that's where the blade was! You know those trick walking sticks where they conceal things—little vials of whiskey and rapiers! That's what she-he had!"

Excited, Chris jumped to his feet. "That's it! That's it exactly! The old bastard!"

"Now tell me," said Kate, reaching for a piece of motel stationery and a pen, "what did she look like? What was she wearing? Exactly what did she-he say to you?"

Chris sat back down and closed his eyes in an effort to re-create the encounter. "Clothes? Droopy, saggy. No color."

"Hat? Shoes?" prompted Kate.

"Shoes I think were high-topped sneakers. Hat . . . boy, that was really something! Had a bunch of stuff on it and hung down around her-his ears."

"What kind of stuff?"

"Aw, Kate, I don't know. Fur-like mice all around the crown."

Kate stood up. "Chris, you underwhelm me. So precise. Can you tell me what she-he said?"

He pondered. "Well, she went marching up to the room door, but I stopped her. I said, 'Hold on, no visitors,' or something sharp like that. She said she was the patient's blood kin and she had a right. I said 'Doctor's orders' or something. She still had a hold on the doorknob. So I aimed my camera and said anybody going in that room had to be photographed. That stopped her."

"But not long enough," said Kate. "What did she say?"

"I told you. All about her religion that holds it a sin to have your image on film. I didn't want her sinning, bad shape as she was in already."

"Nice of you," Kate said grimly. "So you let her go in?"

"Yeah. I walked down the hall to the drink machine and then all hell broke loose. Screaming and everybody running."

"Did you see her-him?"

"Yeah, the old broad in the hat came catapulting out of that room and headed for the stairs. Nurses and doctors and people went right past her on the run. Code Blue, a lady in a pink smock told me."

"I guess so," said Kate. "It's what they call it when a patient's heart stops or something."

Kate folded her notes, lifted a hand to tell Chris good night, and went back to her own room. For long moments she sat at the little desk the Big Rock afforded, looking with unseeing eyes at the nearly blank piece of paper. She began a list of people who might have some-how had something to do with the murders: starting with the people whose names she remembered at Pearlie's, going to Addie Armentrout, the state house quartet, the sheriff and his deputy, and finally even Mrs. Charles Land and Mr. Goodman there at the motel. *Goodman*, she thought, staring at the name. What did she know about that name? Suddenly she remembered. Representative Goodman, the verbose fellow from the peach belt, one of those who had fled when the wet-suited apparition had come up out of the Blue Hole. She wrote down by his name the well-worn southern question: *Any kin?*

She thought of the list as she divested the girls of their dirty blue jeans and pulled blankets over them. She was pulling off her own when she thought she and Edie and Edie's mother were the only people in town who hadn't made the list. She went back to the desk and wrote down Mrs. Putnam's name.

CHAPTER SIX

ON MONDAY MORNING Kate and the girls, show-
ered and shampooed but still wearing jeans and shirts
with the evidence of Sunday's dire happenings on them,
approached the desk to check out. Mrs. Land was back,
this time wearing a hand-knit powder-blue skirt with a
matching sweater, and silver earrings and necklace
instead of pearls.

She greeted them cordially. "On your way back to
Atlanta, are you?"

"Not quite yet," Kate said. "I want to run over to
Chattanooga to the courthouse first."

"Ah, of course. You think land sales and transfers will
help you solve murders."

Kate hesitated. "I don't know. Do you think so?"

"What do I know?" Mrs. Land asked, rolling her pretty
blue eyes. "I just work here. What have you got for a
motive? If it isn't sex or power it is usually money, I find

from reading my murder mysteries. And around here land is about all the money that's left."

Kate brightened. "You could tell me things, I know. I'd appreciate help."

"Why don't you call Edith Putnam—mother, not daughter—and ask her to ride over to Chattanooga with you? I bet she'd like to get away."

Kate was about to explain that Mrs. Putnam had practially thrown her out of the house the night before, but Mrs. Land had dialed the number and was handing her the phone. No mention of a five-minute limit from this desk clerk.

Mrs. Putnam answered promptly, accepted promptly, and asked Kate to pick her up back of the high school. She would, she said, be waiting inside the back door.

"How funny," Kate said, handing the phone back.

Mrs. Land quirked a dark eyebrow.

"I just didn't think she'd go," Kate said, shrugging. She decided not to mention the high school as a pickup place and she really didn't know why. Instead, she said, "Mr. Goodman who works here, is he related to Representative Trent Goodman?"

"Son," Mrs. Land said. "Trent owns this elegant hostelry. Junior is supposed to look after it and I'm supposed to look after him." She grinned and added, "Don't tell anybody I said that. I need this job."

"I won't," Kate said, collecting the girls from the lobby drink machine and marshaling them toward the parking lot.

The Mrs. Putnam who waited inside the high school

166

hall for her was a different person from the warm assured woman who had been so welcoming on Saturday night. She seemed smaller and pale and very nervous. She got in Kate's car and locked the door, forgetting to speak to the little girls until they patted her shoulder and spoke to her.

"Oh, hi, honey," she said. And then to Kate, "Take off, let's go. I hate wasting time."

"Me, too," said Kate, whipping out of the school parking lot and onto the highway. When she felt well under way she said conversationally, "Who's after us? Who are we running from?"

"I'll tell you, but wait . . . don't turn here. Keep on up the mountain!"

"That's the Chattanooga turn," said Kate. "You don't want to go there?"

"No-o! And you don't need to. I'll tell you all you need to know."

Kate wanted to snap, *Start telling me, then!* but the frightened face of the little woman stopped her. She said gently, "When you get your breath."

"Thank you," said Mrs. Putnam. "When we get there—"

"Where?" asked Kate.

"Up to Dr. Polgrim's. I'll show you."

"You mean Dr. Poultice? I know the way there."

Mrs. Putnam sighed and settled back in the seat and closed her eyes.

Kate passed the Sweet Love community and found Dr. Poultice's neat little house with no trouble. He heard them drive in and came out in the yard to meet them.

His old face was troubled and he offered none of the usual pleasantries but opened the door on Mrs. Putnam's side and said quietly, "Go on in the house." To Kate he said, "Pull over there back of the shed. Close. It won't be seen from the road."

"Why we hiding, Miss Kate?" asked Sheena.

"Beats me," said Kate. "I hope we'll soon find out. You girls be very quiet."

"Then will we go to Rock City?" asked Kim Sue.

"We'll see," said Kate, still thinking of going on to Chattanooga.

The old man had settled Mrs. Putnam by his coal fire with a cup of herb tea, and he got out cups and a pot of tea for Kate and the girls.

"You tell her, Doctor," Mrs. Putnam said respectfully. "You know the story."

"Yes." The old man sighed. "Only too well. I told you, I believe, that this country is still rich in every kind of mineral, in coal and in lead. Many entrepreneurs have thought to resume mining through the years and for one reason or another given it up. But in the last few months a Tennessee company has been very active buying up land, first across the state line and then on our side. We heard they were going to try strip-mining and that's when Turn Pickett got busy. But it wasn't just that he feared his ancestors' old lands would be ruined again, it was worse than that."

"They started buying up everything in town," Mrs. Putnam said. "I don't even own my own home anymore. They said they needed it for some kind of big church they were planning. They offered me quite a lot of money and told me I could stay there till they were ready to build. I didn't tell Edie. I thought she was probably going to marry Turn and I was hoping to surprise her with a nice chunk of money."

"You signed papers?" Kate asked.

"Oh, yes, all notarized and everything."

"But you haven't collected any money yet?"

"Oh, no." Mrs. Putnam looked as if she might cry. "After Turn's death I changed my mind and told them so—but they wouldn't let me out of it!"

"Who wouldn't?" asked Kate.

"PawPaw," Mrs. Putnam whispered. "That's why he was at my house last night."

"He and...?"

"Trent Goodman, Jr."

"They're in this together?"

"PawPaw is a resident of Tennessee with a home there," Dr. Poultice put in. "He's the one who formed this mysterious company north of the line and started buying up property. Trent Goodman is the leader in some strange religious cult. He wants to build a big church complex in the valley, which would take in most of Rising Fawn." The old doctor made a face. "I think he had in mind something like that one in Waco, Texas, until the FBI wiped that out."

"But the mines?" put in Kate. "Why would he want all that country?"

"I'm going to tell you," the old man said. "That's why they killed Turn Pickett. Those underground tunnels and passages were going to be connected to the church. We didn't know that until some of my friends up at Sweet Love came to see me. They don't seem very energetic people"—he allowed himself a wry smile—"but they get around a lot at night and some of the underground passages lend themselves admirably to whiskey making. One night a couple of my friends found a very large cache of rifles, machine guns, and boxes of ammunition and other explosives. They didn't know what to do with it, so they came to see me."

"Church supplies?" Kate said sarcastically.

Dr. Poultice nodded. "More useful than hymnbooks and missals," he said. "Anyhow, to continue, I wanted Turn's help, but he was in Atlanta and I didn't think we should take a chance on waiting. My friends from Sweet Love and I took my truck and theirs and went into the mine late at night and hauled everything out and brought it here and secured it in a cave back of their waterfall."

Kate had a mental picture of that hideaway, with dirty clothes a-washing under the falling water and concealing the mouth of the cave. Edie had called it the Sweet Love community's Laundromat, but it seemed to be much, much more.

"When did you tell Turn?"

The old man sighed and was silent. Tears came to his eyes and he wiped them on the sleeve of his work shirt.

"The night he got home from Atlanta. He often brought me supplies from town and if it was late he would leave them inside the door and go on. That night I

was awake waiting for him. He must have called and con-
fronted one of them with that information."

"They didn't need to kill him!" Kate cried.

"They may have thought he would report their arsenal
or that he knew where it was hidden and wouldn't tell,"
Dr. Poultice said. "I don't know any more about it than
that which I have told you."

That which, Kate wanted to tell him, left a lot of
unanswered questions.

"You see, my dear," said Mrs. Putnam, looking very
sad, "you won't get any information at the courthouse. I
don't think there's a record there yet of a single of these
land transactions, and they were many, including the Big
Rock Motel, among others."

"If it isn't recorded and you haven't been paid anything, I think you can get your house back," Kate said.
"Do you have a lawyer? Let's go see him!"

Mrs. Putnam's lawyer had an office in the neighboring
town of Summerville. Kate drove her there, wishing she
could cut loose and go seek some answers on her own.
But the little woman had been kind to her and Kim Sue
and Sheena, and Kate couldn't cut her loose until Edie
got home from school and could look after her.

"Is it PawPaw you're afraid of?" Kate asked as they
entered the lawyer's office.

"Not so much PawPaw himself," Mrs. Putnam said.
"It's the people he can round up to do his meanness.
Last night he brought Trent Goodman, Jr., to my house.

I've known that boy several years and he's always had a streak of violence in him. I think he would have hurt me if PawPaw had told him to."

"How about Lorena?" Kate asked. "Who killed her, and why?"

"I don't know," Mrs. Putnam said. "She was close to them. Typed all their papers and served as their notary public. I always thought they gave her that fur coat as a kind of payoff."

"That reminds me of something else I was going to do in Chattanooga," Kate said. "I had the name of the furrier from the label in Lorena's coat and I was going to call and see if there was a record of the sale. I'll find a phone and call while you're talking to your lawyer."

It didn't take the young lawyer long to tell Mrs. Putnam she and half a dozen other people in Rising Fawn had been victims of fraud. And it didn't take Kate long to trace the former well-respected Chattanooga furrier. He had retired and gone out of business, selling some of his leftover stock to a costume company.

Mrs. Putnam came out of the lawyer's office smiling and Kate came out of the telephone booth in the lobby laughing.

"Lorena's coat was rented!" she cried.

By the time they got back to Rising Fawn, Edie was home from school, and Kate dropped off her mother at their house. Sheena and Kim Sue were clamoring for lunch, and Kate thought she had figured out most of the Scratch Ankle happenings. She picked up hamburgers for the girls and drove straight to the sheriff's office.

He was in conference with PawPaw once more. This time he insisted that the big man stay in his office while he went out to speak to Kate, who left the girls reading old comic books in the outer office.

"I have him for you if you want to ask him some questions," he murmured to Kate. "I can't make him answer you, but you can give it a try."

"Thanks, Sheriff," Kate said, smiling at him. "I think I have some answers for him instead of questions."

She entered the office, took a chair opposite PawPaw, and began pleasantly enough. "How are you feeling after your ordeal in the well?"

"Aw, great! Great!" he said. "You can't keep a good man down. Or, as somebody up at Pearlie's said this morning, you can't shaft a shafter!" He laughed immoderately.

Kate waited for the sheriff to come in and take a seat. Then she said, "I guess we know about your dealings with Mr. Goodman, the land, the proposed church, and all those guns you all were stockpiling in the mines!"

PawPaw's red face went white. The sheriff was very quiet.

"When Turn told you he had found the arsenal and was going to report it to the authorities, you decided to kill him. Why?"

"Oh, I didn't . . . I wouldn't a done that!" cried PawPaw. "It was Junior, Goodman's boy." His eyes appealed to the sheriff. "You know how wild he gets. We just told him—"

Suddenly Kate remembered the motel clerk's khaki pants. *Smokey the Bear wears khaki*, she remembered, and she said quickly, "Sheriff, Representative Goodman's son ... I think he's the one who has been playing Smokey in the woods. I bet if you searched his room at the motel you'd find a ranger's broad-brimmed hat and other Smokey stuff."

"Yeah," said PawPaw eagerly. "You know Junior. He likes to play games."

"Wait a minute, PawPaw," the sheriff said. "We want to get this down right. Byron, bring a notebook."

The deputy came in with a notebook and a tape recorder.

"Raise your hand, PawPaw."

"I ain't gon' do this, Jeff," PawPaw protested. "I'm a innocent party. Trent got me into this and he's a powerful legislator and I'm gon' be stuck with it. You know I wouldn't a hurt Lorena, not for the world!"

"When she found out that fur coat you gave her was rented..." Kate said softly.

PawPaw attempted a laugh. "It was a joke."

"Is that when she told you she wasn't gon' give back the bills of sale for that real estate you were acquiring?"

"Well, she did act unreasonable about that. Made Trent and Junior pretty mad."

"And so they beat her up and still didn't get the papers, so Junior decided to finish the job with a rapier in a walking cane at the hospital."

The sheriff stood up suddenly and walked to the big iron safe in the corner of the room. He fumbled with the combination and finally the tumblers fell into place with a satisfactory bump and he opened the heavy iron door.

When he turned again, he had a big folder in his hand. He sat down and showed it to Kate.

"'Private, Personal Property of Lorena Cumby. Do not open.'"

Kate waited while he opened it. A dozen agreements to sell—little houses, farmland, the motel, one church, all signed and notarized.

"Well, good God-amighty!" cried PawPaw.

"Nifty hiding place," said Kate.

The sheriff smiled at her and said, "Byron, show PawPaw to the guest room."

Kate took the little girls shopping for clean clothes and then to see Rock City. When they swung back by Rising Fawn, both Trent and his son had been arrested and FBI agents had been introduced to the arsenal back of Sweet Love's waterfall.

Representative Banks had come walking in from a warm and congenial evening spent with some of the young ladies from Pearlie's Café. And Addie Armentrout was in the sheriff's office crying her head off.

"I know Trent Junior done it! I know!" she cried. "When he gits mad he kills things." She held up an embroidered doily that enclosed the body of her mynah bird, its neck wrung. "That night I let him use one of my cabins to meet a lady friend and . . . " her eyes fell on Kate, "*she* come instid! Hit made him mad!"

"And rightfully so," Kate murmured.

The sheriff walked Kate to the front steps, where he thanked her warmly for her help, promised to keep her informed about the case, and hugged each of the Gandy sisters. "If they let me keep this office," he said, "I'm gon' make deputies out of all three of you."

Kate started to say it was an honor she thought she could forgo, but she thought of something else.

"Sheriff, that hat Junior wore to get in the hospital . . . if you can find it, save it for evidence. I think he may have decorated it with stuffed mice that were killed the same way he killed Addie's mynah bird."